MY SINGLE-VERSARY

LAUREN BLAKELY

ALSO BY LAUREN BLAKELY

Big Rock Series

Big Rock

Mister O

Well Hung

Full Package

Joy Ride

Hard Wood

Happy Endings Series

My Single-Versary

A Wild Card Kiss

Shut Up and Kiss Me

Kismet

Rules of Love Series

The Rules of Friends with Benefits (A Prequel Novella)

The Virgin Rule Book

The Virgin Game Plan

The Virgin Replay

The Virgin Scorecard

Men of Summer Series

Scoring With Him

Winning With Him

All In With Him

The Guys Who Got Away Series

Dear Sexy Ex-Boyfriend

The What If Guy

Thanks for Last Night

The Dream Guy Next Door

The Gift Series

The Engagement Gift

The Virgin Gift

The Decadent Gift

The Extravagant Series

One Night Only

One Exquisite Touch

My One-Week Husband

MM Standalone Novels

A Guy Walks Into My Bar

One Time Only

The Bromance Zone

The Heartbreakers Series

Once Upon a Real Good Time

Once Upon a Sure Thing

Once Upon a Wild Fling

Boyfriend Material

Asking For a Friend

Sex and Other Shiny Objects

One Night Stand-In

Lucky In Love Series

Best Laid Plans

The Feel Good Factor

Nobody Does It Better

Unzipped

Always Satisfied Series

Satisfaction Guaranteed

Instant Gratification

Overnight Service

Never Have I Ever

PS It's Always Been You

Special Delivery

The Sexy Suit Series

Lucky Suit

Birthday Suit

From Paris With Love

Wanderlust

Part-Time Lover

One Love Series

The Sexy One

The Only One

The Hot One

The Knocked Up Plan

Come As You Are

Sports Romance

Most Valuable Playboy

Most Likely to Score

Standalones

Stud Finder

The V Card

The Real Deal

Unbreak My Heart

The Break-Up Album

The Caught Up in Love Series

The Pretending Plot (previously called *Pretending He's Mine*)

The Dating Proposal

The Second Chance Plan (previously called *Caught Up In Us*)

The Private Rehearsal (previously called *Playing With Her Heart*)

Seductive Nights Series

Night After Night

After This Night

One More Night

A Wildly Seductive Night

ABOUT

How to survive a break up -- swear off men for a year.

How to celebrate a successful year long man cleanse -- treat myself to a solo tropical vacation.

It's me time on my single-versary, so you'll find me snorkeling, sight-seeing, and zip lining by the sea. No man companions needed, thank you very much.

Until the hot, hunky and charming adventure tour guide shows up at surfboard yoga. And Caleb's got me thinking about new uses for downward facing dog.

But indulging in an island fling that'll surely put me on the path to heartbreak again is definitely not on the my single-versary agenda.

At least, it shouldn't be on the agenda.

MY SINGLE-VERSARY

By Lauren Blakely

Want to be the first to learn of sales, new releases, preorders and special freebies? Sign up for my VIP mailing list here!

PROLOGUE

Skyler

At some point in your twenties, everyone in your social circle begins pairing off and pairing up. It's a checklist—one minute you and your three roommates (because how else is a woman supposed to live in the city?) are rescuing perfectly salvageable bookcases from the curbside, and the next, you're buying thirty-dollar bottles of wine as housewarming gifts. Your girl-power pub quiz team becomes co-ed, then splits off into pairs, and then suddenly you look up and everyone you know is counting down to thirty like it's New Year's Eve and they have to find someone to kiss before the ball drops and they're partnerless at midnight.

The horror . . .

Not that your friends want to leave you out in the cold. No one loves love more than someone *in* love, and they want all their friends to be just as happy as they are. All my friends know a guy. Or their guy knows a guy.

But I made a decision after my last heartbreak—to take a full year off from dating.

I went on a man cleanse. One I desperately needed to reset myself.

I've resisted romance. Each time my friends said, "Can I set you up?" or "I know a guy," I dropped some coins in a jar.

And every day I stayed off the dating apps, I fed the piggy bank.

My reward? A "me" trip.

To celebrate.

Even if that "me" trip happens to coincide with my cousin's wedding. I'll just breeze through that, then hit up the bar, or the spa, or the line of shops all calling my name to indulge in me, me, me.

Here I am. One year, no dating. Achievement unlocked.

At least, that's the plan.

1

SKYLER

With one silver ballet flat in hand, I open my door for Katie before she has a chance to knock. "Come in. The mate to my shoe has pulled a vanishing act."

My friend stands with her fist raised for another second or two, then follows me into the apartment, closing the door behind her. "Hmm . . . maybe the universe is trying to tell you something, Skyler. To buy new shoes?"

I fish out the missing footwear from under the sofa. "Or it's telling me to put my shoes away before I fall asleep during the latest Webflix romantic comedy."

Katie idly picks up the large glass jar from the kitchen island, turning it over so the coins inside jingle loudly. "Skyler, sweetie, you could crack someone's skull open with this! It's that heavy."

"Hawaii heavy." I slip on the rejoined pair of ballet flats, take the jar of loose change from her, and replace it on the counter with a thud. "I've resisted Tinder, Bumble, and Match every day to save up for this trip."

Katie rubs her hands together. "So, are you ready to go?"

"Ready to go to Hawaii? Absolutely." I sling my purse over my shoulder and lead the way out, locking up behind us. "Ready to go bathing suit shopping?" I waggle a noncommittal hand. "Debatable."

Katie tsks as she takes out her car keys. "Says the professional shopper."

I pop open the passenger door of her rented Tesla—she's in town from Los Angeles, where she runs her yoga empire. "People hire me when they don't have the time or inclination to shop for themselves. Searching for something to fit me and my budget is totally different."

We both climb in, and Katie turns to me, a challenging brow raised. "Don't tell me you're intimidated by a few items of swimwear?"

"It's not the swimwear that scares me. It's the fluorescent lighting in the dressing rooms."

She's laughing as she starts the car and heads toward the heart of San Francisco's best boutiques. "Cheap and chicken."

"I am not cheap," I protest, which makes her

laugh harder as we make our way to Fillmore Street.

Once in the shop, Katie drafts a salesperson into raiding the racks with her. They sort through tops and bottoms with efficiency that I envy as a personal stylist, and when the saleswoman has armfuls of itty-bitty items, she ushers me into a dressing room.

I thank her, and with an encouraging smile, she says, "Good luck. Let me know if you need another size."

Ugh. I need to not wear bikinis.

Katie taps her chin with one finger as she eyes the array of nylon and spandex hanging before us in the dressing room. When her gaze lands on what she wants, though, she knows it immediately. "Try that one." She points. "I have a good feeling about it."

I stare at the scraps of fabric dubiously. "The one with pasties for the top and dental floss for the bottom?"

Katie challenges me with a deadpan look. "You *did* say you wanted a brand-new style of bathing suit. Surely, a floss-bottom would qualify."

"Yes, as a new form of sartorial torture."

"You're not wrong." She flicks through the options and stops on a fuchsia two-piece. "How about this cute little number?"

I pick up the suit and try to make sense of it.

"Which is the top and which is the bottom? I can't tell."

Katie makes a giant show of taking the suit from me and putting it on the "no" hanger. *"Help me shop for a bathing suit, Katie,"* she mutters. *"It'll be a blast. I won't be a total pain in the butt."*

"Hey, unfair!" I wave at the dental-floss thong. *"This* looks like a pain in the butt."

"Slam dunk." Katie makes a grudging rim-shot sound effect.

I pick up another offender. *"This,* on the other hand, is so high-waisted it looks like a pull-up diaper."

"But that's trendy. Isn't it?"

I hang the monstrosity on the "no" rack—with prejudice. "Not all trends are *good* trends."

"Hey, here's an idea. How about you wear one of those swim dresses from a century ago? That will be *très* sexy."

"Hmm . . . maybe with some bloomers to give some shape to a pancake-flat butt. And some ruffles here"—I gesture to my chest area—"to make the most of microscopic breasts. We don't all have perfectly proportioned bodies like our beautiful friends."

"Pfft. And some of us don't have perfect noses, adorable freckles, or dimples, like *our* friends. So embrace your you-ness."

"Dimples are irrelevant," I scoff. "I don't put my dimples in a bathing suit."

Katie bursts into laughter. "That sounds like exactly what you would put in a bathing suit."

I laugh too. Katie's humor is hard to resist. "Fine. You win."

She claps her hands. "Yay! Does that mean you'll actually let me find a bikini to put your dimples in?"

With a groan, I picture myself on a beach wearing a few scraps of Lycra. "Or here's a thought—I could skip swimming. Skip sunbathing. I could go on a sightseeing tour. No need for bathing suits or spas or beaches or sunset cruises . . ."

"Skyler," she says, no joking in her gentle reprimand this time. "Remember what this trip represents? You made it through a full year of no romance. You saved your money. This is your reward after all those—"

"Failed relationships where I totally lost sight of myself?"

Soberly, she nods. "Yes. This trip is a celebration of you."

I fidget, uncomfortable with the tough love, even though I appreciate it.

"Have you got an outfit for the ceremony yet?" she asks, her voice a little kinder, a little gentler.

"Yes," I reply, because while this trip is a

celebration of me, it's also been timed to coincide with my cousin Trish's Maui wedding. "Mom says she hopes the wedding will inspire me to tie the knot, but between you and me, I think she wants me to go so she'll have someone to scam on guys with."

Katie laughs dryly. "Yeah, there are too many things wrong with that last sentence to count."

"You're telling me," I say, but I smile, because while Mom is man crazy, she's also my mom, and I love her to pieces.

"But the wedding is only *one day*. The rest of the trip is about pampering yourself with beachside cabana massages and afternoon daiquiris by the pool. It's time to treat yourself the way you've never had any man treat you—the way you deserve."

I draw a deep breath, trying to pin down my hesitation. "It still feels strange—and as uncomfortable as a thong bikini."

"That's called change," Katie says. "You need to get out of your comfort zone. Do the hard things, starting with trying on at least one bikini."

I nod, decisive. I've spent the last year making my own happiness, learning to be comfortable in myself. This reward is part of that. "You're right. Let's do it."

"Yes!" She bounces on her toes. "Cue the

dressing room montage!"

And here we go. Off, on, off, on with the suits, Katie giving thumbs-ups and thumbs-downs, whisking away rejects and thrusting new contenders over the door.

Just when I'm at my limit, I emerge in one last suit, and she takes a look and exclaims, "And we have a winner!"

"Thank God!" I sag against the dressing room door. "Talk about doing the hard stuff."

"It was worth it. That suit looks fab." She gestures to the mirror. "Go ahead. Tell me I'm wrong."

I glance at my bikini-clad image. I love the sapphire color and the way it looks with my auburn hair, hazel eyes, and the aforementioned dimples . . . aflush from the effort of wiggling into strips of elastic and string.

"You're not wrong," I say. "Even if I feel like I just swam across the bay."

She laughs. "How would you know? You hate the ocean. And swimming. And any physical activity that can't be done at the gym."

As soon as she says it, the circuits link up with a flash and a spark.

Bing! Light-bulb moment.

"That's it! That's what I need to do."

Katie blinks. "Go swimming?"

"Yes! Or snorkeling. Or zip-lining. Or anything that's not my jam. I can pamper myself at the spa here at home. Instead, when I go to Maui, I should give myself an experience I would never ordinarily do."

"You're going to reward yourself by doing something you don't like?"

"I know it sounds paradoxical, Katie, but it *feels* right. As good as I feel in this bikini. It's time to get out of my comfort zone."

"I should create a class for that." Katie taps her chin, as if thinking of a new session to add to her business empire. "I could call it *Yoga for people who want to get out of their comfort zone.*"

"You should. And if we lived closer, I would absolutely take that class," I reply. "But for now, I'm going to start with this trip. Let the single-versary adventures begin."

The sapphire-colored bikini is a done deal, and so is my brilliant plan for my single-versary celebration.

2

CALEB

Being your own boss has good points and bad, but being your own boss in Maui means afternoon surf breaks, and that counts for a lot. Ocean breezes, the rush of the surf onto the beach—taking a break from answering email when the temptation of the waves becomes too much to resist . . . I have it good.

I shake the water from my hair and load my board in the back of my Jeep and head back to the house. I start a pot of coffee before I go to change, stripping out of my wetsuit and tugging on board shorts and a T-shirt— Hawaiian lifestyle is the literal best.

On the way to my attached home office, I stop to pour two mugs of Kona Peaberry and bring one to my buddy Brady at his desk.

I nod to the spreadsheet on his computer screen and the weather forecast on his tablet.

"If you're trying to make me feel guilty for grabbing a surf break, it won't work," I say.

"Nah. I'd have gone with you if I wasn't trying to find a guide to fill in for Tom's tour that starts this weekend. We're fully booked."

I stop mid-sip, lowering the mug. "What happened to Tom? I thought he had a stomach bug."

Brady shakes his head. "Nope. Texted from the hospital. Full-blown appendicitis."

Grabbing my phone, I check my messages. "Dammit. He's probably in surgery by now."

"Yeah. We sent a nice potted plant, by the way."

"Thoughtful of us," I say, setting a reminder to check in with him, even if things get busy. "But this weekend . . .?"

He holds up a wait-a-minute finger and then swipes on his tablet. "I just sent you the updated schedule." My phone pings, and I open the link. "I've got everything covered but the five-day adventure tour. I'm busy with surf camp both days."

"No worries," I say. "I wasn't planning to lead a tour next week, so I can do it."

"You sure?" he asks. "I wanted Tom to take this group because he's good with the haters."

"And I'm not?" I make a *gimme* motion with my hand, ready for him to dish up all the details. "What have you got for me?"

"A last-minute addition." He picks up his tablet to read. "Solo guest. Woman named Skyler. Says she's never snorkeled but, to paraphrase, 'Knows she hates it with a passion and can't wait for us to convince her otherwise.'"

I chuckle. "At least we know what we're up against."

Most guests are eager to do something they can't in their day-to-day lives, whether it's the first time or the fiftieth. But every now and then, we get passengers who, for whatever reason, seem determined not to have a good time, no matter what.

Which is a shame—there's so much to enjoy about Hawaii.

A few of the jellyfish will thoroughly mess up your day, but as long as you avoid those, you're golden.

"So, you do surf camp, and I'll take the adventure tour and Ms. I Hate Snorkeling," I tell Brady, typing my name into the schedule. "I love changing people's minds about adventure sports. That's why I started this gig in the first place."

Brady leans back in his chair with a smirk. "It's not so you could surf and hike and get paid for it?"

"That's just a perk." I point to my almost empty mug. "Like locally roasted Kona and sunshine."

"Speaking of things that *aren't* perks . . ." He sips his own coffee. "Remember that guy you didn't want to hire because he had an 'opportunist vibe'?"

I don't think my people instincts merit finger quotes, but whatever. "He went to work as a guide for Excursions, didn't he? What did he do? Hook up with a guest?"

"Gave her the whole business, apparently. Led her on with romance under the stars, long walks along the ocean, 'never felt like this before' sweet nothings—and then cut her loose. She left the mother of all scathing reviews on Travelocity, complaining about the boat, the staff, the facilities . . ."

"Ouch." Hard luck for Excursions, but their guy broke one of the cardinal rules of tour-guiding.

The first is *Come back with the same number of people you left with.*

The second is *No canoodling on the job.*

"Romance with clients is always a terrible idea," I say. "The Mia situation taught me that."

Brady nods. "You don't need another koala of a girl clinging to you."

I shudder at the memory. "I don't. But let's be fair to marsupials— koalas *are* adorable."

Thing is, even when everyone's on board, a tour hookup is never going to lead anywhere—nowhere worth risking your business or reputation. For one thing, getting cozy with a guest while you should be paying attention to your other clients is dangerous.

But a vacation romance is only a recipe for heartache. It will mess you up worse than any box jelly, so the only thing to do is avoid them altogether.

3

SKYLER

"Ladies and gentlemen, welcome to Maui," the flight attendant says as we taxi to the gateway. "We hope you enjoyed your flight. Local time is two-thirty, and the temperature is a balmy eighty-two degrees."

Kahului Airport pulls me into the island spirit as soon as I exit the plane. It's busy with pale tourists arriving, sunburned ones departing, and everywhere I look are explosions of color. Skylights and palms blend indoors and out until I can't tell the difference.

I find my suitcase at the baggage carousel and exit the airport, fully savoring the balmy eighty-two degrees the flight attendant promised and drinking in the Pacific air. The breeze toys with my hair and smells entirely different than San Francisco.

It smells like vacation.

Hello, single-versary, here I am.

I hail a taxi that's making a circuit of the arrival gates. When it stops, I greet the driver, then toss my bags in the back seat and slide in beside them. Gotta love tropical getaways—sundresses and sandals make luggage light.

"Where you headed?" asks the cabbie as I click in my seat belt.

"Well, I'm going to a wedding tonight," I answer cheerfully. "And then tomorrow, I'm going to get out of my comfort zone for my single-versary."

"Single-versary?" He glances at me in the rearview mirror, his dark brown eyes crinkling with a grin. "Is that something you do at karaoke?"

"Nope. It's a year of being happily single while everyone I know seems to be posting engagement pictures and cutesy save-the-date announcements."

"Congratulations." There's a honk behind us as we idle, and he smiles widely at me. "But I meant what hotel are you headed to."

"Oh." Of course he did. "The Hilton, please."

The taxi pulls away from the airport, and the driver strikes up a conversation. "So, the whole single thing—that's awesome. Maybe you can have an island fling here. I'm off after six."

"Thank you, but no," I say politely. "The point is I'm trying to *not* date."

"Sure, sure. But seriously, I have a Door-Dash shift this afternoon. You want dinner? I recommend Joe's Surf and Turf for their local halibut. I can have it to the Hilton in less than ten minutes. You change your mind about having company with dinner, just order the 'something on the side' special. But I can only stay for twenty minutes."

I have no plans to take him up on that, but his salesmanship *is* impressive. "I'll consider it. Do I get a promo code?"

"Sure thing." His eyebrows wiggle in the rearview mirror. "It's Double O."

That's a hell of an offer.

Turning it down has got to be worth *at least* the price of a halibut dinner added to the reward jar.

At the wedding that night, my cousin Trish looks amazing in a simple sundress-style wedding dress with a hibiscus in her hair. Blake, her groom, gazes at her with love in his eyes, clearly besotted.

They trade "I dos" at sunset on the beach, and it's insanely romantic.

Even my man-cleansed heart flutters as he

kisses the bride like he will indeed cherish her always.

A little later, the reception is going strong inside the tent on the hotel grounds. Near the dance floor, I catch up with Sierra and Clementine, some friends from San Francisco.

Sierra's been making eyes at a strapping, sexy baseball player, and she catches us up on what's going on with the star closer from the San Francisco Cougars.

It's a delish story, and I can't wait to hear how it all shakes out. "You do have a just-been-fucked look about you," I tease, gesturing to her glowing skin.

"I will take that as the compliment it is," she says.

Clementine turns to me, all big eyes and eager voice. "And what about you? Will you indulge in some sunset yada yada yada here on your solo vacay?"

"Nope. I'm sticking to my diet," I say, then give them the scoop on my resolution.

"Good luck with that," Sierra says.

"You have the doubtful sound of a woman who's getting a little action," I tease.

"Then as long as you don't get a little action, you'll be fine sticking to your diet," she says.

"Or a *big* action," Clementine adds.

"And really, that's the best kind," Sierra puts in.

"You two are not helpful," I warn.

"Were we supposed to be?" Sierra tosses back.

"On that note, good luck," Clementine says, and Sierra echoes her.

Maybe they sound a bit doubtful, but I'm happy.

After all, I'm in Hawaii, the reception food is amazing, and the wine has me loosened up enough that I cheer enthusiastically when the DJ announces it's time to toss the bouquet.

"Who's going to make that catch?" he calls into the mic. "All the single ladies, raise your arms in the air! Whoop whoop!"

Trish gets into position with her back to the dance floor, laughing as her bridesmaids shout at her to throw it their way and they elbow each other for a prime spot.

I get an elbow in my own ribs and see that my mom has *somehow* managed to be right beside me at the opportune time. "Come on, Skyler! Let's get out there and go for it!"

I giggle at her enthusiasm. "*You* go for it, Mom."

"No, we both have to do it. Mother-daughter tag team."

There's no time to argue. Mom and I charge into the throng just as the DJ counts down, "Three, two, one! Here she goes!"

The bride lobs the bouquet, and the gaggle

of women turns into a rugby match complete with high heels and cocktail dresses. We scrabble and gasp, and then someone squeals, "I got it!" and holds the flowers high in victory.

Mom finds me as the clump disperses, still staggering with laughter. "Sky! You were *right there*. I thought for sure you had it."

"You wanted me to dive for it, Mom? I didn't want it that badly."

"Everybody wants to catch the bouquet." She blows a fallen strand of hair from her face. "*I* wanted to catch the bouquet. I trained for months. It was there at the tip of my fingers and then bounced off."

"Curses." I snap my fingers. "Just have to try again at one of the nine weddings for which I'm saving the date."

She sighs. "Speak for yourself. You have all the wedding invitations. I just get birth announcements for my friends' *grandchildren*."

Her emphasis has me raising my hands in surrender. "Don't even go there, Mom."

"I know." Another sigh. "I just want you to be happy, Skyler."

I remind her gently, "I *am* happy, Mom. I'm happy being single."

"But look at all these handsome grooms-men." She points across the way. "And look at that. That silver fox is Harold Armstrong, your cousin's uncle's friend. He's retired and single. Plus, I hear he can still drive at night."

"Quite the catch for a sexy senior citizen."

"Hush." She gives my arm a teasing pinch. "Don't tell a soul I'm sixty-five. I'm forever forty-nine. In fact, maybe we should pretend I'm your older sister."

I choke. "My *twenty-years-older* sister."

"Don't cockblock me, sweetheart." She's target-locked on Harold Armstrong, eligible bachelor. "I'm going in."

"Good luck, sis." She's ridiculous, and I love her too much to be angry at her nudging me altar-ward.

I say good night to Sierra and Clementine, wish Trish and Blake well, and go to my room alone.

It all feels just right.

* * *

In the morning, I'm ready to tackle the day. After I get dressed I make my way to the beach. I FaceTime Katie as I walk across the sand, showing off the view on my phone. "Good morning from paradise! That's Hawaiian paradise, not the afterlife. Just clarifying, since today I take on the ocean, aka that giant caldron of sea creatures, aka Things That Want to Eat You."

"Yes, I'm sure the fish will find you tasty."

"I did slather on some coconut lotion this morning, so I'm probably all tropical and yummy."

"Then, I hope they enjoy their breakfast of you," she teases, as I swing the screen to dock where I'm meeting the group. "And that's the boat that will carry us out over the abyss."

"Speaking of tasty, who is that stone-cold fox by the boat? Is he on your tour?" Her eyes go wide as the sky.

I peer over the screen at the sight in front of me. A tall, tanned drink of man, then I whisper to Katie. "I think that's the skipper of my Island Adventure Tour. This IS a cruel joke, but I will not be tempted," I say, wagging my finger.

She scoffs. "How can you not be tempted? He's, like, movie star good-looking."

"I am strong," I say, walking closer to the matinee idol.

Katie looks doubtful. "What if he takes off his shirt to swim? What if you swoon at the sight, and he has to give you mouth-to-mouth?"

"You don't give mouth-to-mouth for a swoon."

"Well, if *he* swoons, I suggest you offer mouth-to-mouth."

"Enabler," I hiss, then, flinch, quickly bringing the phone closer, to shield my mouth. Who knows if he can read lips? "He's waving at me now. And tapping his watch. Time to go. Say nice things at my funeral if I die a watery death."

"I'll say the fish enjoyed the last meal of you."

4

CALEB

That has to be the snorkel hater on the dock, chatting on her phone. I glimpsed her snapping a selfie or taking a video with the boat in the background.

I also glimpsed a slim figure, tanned and toned legs under sensible shorts, and glorious red hair that would rival a sunset for color. Her profile shows off a cute, upturned nose, and her animated expressions as she talks are kind of adorable.

She doesn't *look* like a nightmare passenger.

She looks as intriguing as her challenge.

But she's also the last guest to board.

I get her attention and smile as I tap my watch. She quickly stuffs her phone in her pocket, and I meet her as she steps onto the boat.

"Hey there," I say with a grin. "You must be Skyler, the snorkel hater."

Her laugh is bright and sweet—not the laugh of someone who's about to make my week difficult. "What gave it away?"

"Your T-shirt," I say. She looks at the design in confusion. It reads: *But first, coffee.* "Studies show that most snorkel haters are coffee lovers."

She cocks her head, hazel eyes lively. "Is the opposite true? Do you hate coffee, since you're a snorkel lover?"

Her nose scrunches up. The most adorable freckles are dotted over her cheeks. "Nah. I'm just a lover."

"Hey, Caleb!" Jimmy, one of my crew, shouts from the deck above. "Where'd you put that cruelty-free sunblock?"

A timely reminder—work first.

"Check under the bench on the deck," I shout over my shoulder. Behind me, I hear Skyler mutter to herself.

"What was that?" I ask when I turn back.

She starts, eyes wide, then clears her throat. "Oh, I was just wondering if you know what to do for swooning."

I frown, wondering if she needs reassurance. "You mean for seasickness or . . .?"

"For lines like"—her voice drops in pitch to mimic mine—*"I'm just a lover."*

Oh, direct hit. I grab my chest like she's shot me and laugh. She doesn't seem like a nightmare—in fact, she's seeming a little dreamier every time she opens her mouth. "Point to you. I'm Caleb, by the way. I'll be your adventure tour guide."

"As you guessed, I'm Skyler." She gives a snappy, sassy salute. "Reporting for snorkel conversion therapy."

I rub my palms together. "I'm ready for the challenge. All the other tour participants are on board. Let me show you where you can stow your tote and then I'll introduce you to the gear."

"Can't wait."

Funny thing is, she sounds like she more than half means it.

* * *

Once we're underway, headed for the snorkeling site down the coast, I check that the other guests, who've all snorkeled before, have everything they need. Before issuing any instructions, I want to give Skyler time to adjust to the feel of the boat skimming across the water, throwing up spray as the hull slaps the surface. She went pale as we left the marina, but her color came back as she focused on other things.

And since one of those things is me, I'm happy to oblige her.

Hauling some of the fins out of the chest, I set them on the deck in front of her, the rubber slapping loudly. "Choose your poison. We've got your basic fin here," I say, picking it up and pointing to the next. "Then this is a sport fin, and we've got those performance fins there."

Skyler stands with her arms folded and her hip cocked. "What's a performance fin? More to the point, how does the fin improve your performance?"

Straight-faced, I tell her, "Fish do appreciate when you make the effort to act your best."

"Oh, sure. I want to give the fish a good show." A sexy, cheeky grin curls her luscious lips. "Except isn't the idea that the fish are the attraction? I could watch *boring* fish in my dentist's office—shouldn't they be putting on a show for me?"

"They will if you wear the performance fin."

"Then performance fin it is. I'd hate to go through all this trouble for nothing."

I put away the others, and when I return, she's at the rail, looking at the island as we circle it. Normally, I'd leave a passenger to their thoughts, but, as Brady says, newbies need a lot of hand-holding.

But not *that kind* of hand-holding.

That kind gets you scathing reviews online.

Only, I can't help but wonder what it would be like to have her hands on any part of me, full stop.

I focus on my job, which is to keep her safe and comfortable, as well as to show her and the others a fun time.

"Why didn't you want to snorkel?" I ask without teasing, joining her at the railing. "Did you have a bad experience?"

She gives me a sidelong look as if checking my sincerity, then she sighs. "Don't laugh."

I hold up my hand. "Scout's honor."

Another sigh, even deeper than the first. "I tried it once before. I dated this guy in college, and we went snorkeling in Miami. And . . ."

She pauses like this is tough for her, and I give her time.

"He was big into water sports, so he insisted I go. But I had no clue what to do, and when I asked, he told me to just get in the water and I'd figure it out. 'Nothing can go wrong,' he said."

"Plenty of things can go wrong," I say calmly, despite my anger on her behalf. "What happened?"

"I got nervous and put my feet down on some coral." I hiss in sympathy, and she winces. "Slashed my foot and wound up in the hospital."

"Ouch. Coral is vicious. I'm sorry to hear that."

"I had no idea. Which, I suppose, makes me foolish."

"Nah, you're not foolish." I lighten my tone. "Coral appears pretty, like a lovely ocean friend, but it can hurt like the dickens."

"Right? I had no idea it would sting so badly. And then I suppose you add in my instinctive fear of sharks."

I nod solemnly. "Understandable."

"And those currents that pull you under or sweep you out to sea."

"Not too many of those out here."

She scoffs. "I bet you say that to all the nervous tourists. *Anyway*, that's how I became an anti-snorkeler."

"I accepted your challenge, didn't I? My job now is to make you love snorkeling as much as you love coffee."

"Good luck with that," she says dryly. "Because I really love my coffee."

"Have a little faith. I know what I'm doing. And snorkeling is awesome. It's peaceful and beautiful and eye-opening. And I understand the ocean can be terrifying if you don't spend a lot of time around it. So how about I just stick by you when you go underwater?"

She glances at me in surprise, as if sticking by her would be a hardship. "You'd do that?"

"Of course."

"What about the others?" She glances

toward the bow where a majority of the guests are gathered around Jimmy, who's pointing out various sights on the horizon.

"I've got assistants here. I'll keep an eye on you. I want you to have fun, Skyler, and to enjoy the ocean in a whole new way. And I'm not going to let you go into the water without any instructions."

Her shoulders drop from where they were hunched around her ears. "Thanks. I mean, I didn't think you would, but . . ."

"Hey, you're in the hands of a professional snorkel-lover now." I flash a grin, which she returns. "Let's start with some general tips."

I give her the dos and don'ts of snorkeling, and she's focused in like I'm giving her the answers to *Final Jeopardy*.

She's a quick study, though, and by the time we're anchored and ready to go in the water, and she strips down to her swimsuit—holy shit, that bikini—her nerves seem as much from excitement as fear.

Obviously, I need to give myself some tips of my own.

Do focus on the job.

Don't stare at your guest, no matter how good she looks in that bikini.

Trouble is, rules only keep you on course if you follow them.

5

SKYLER

A fish as shimmery as a sapphire wiggles past me. It's so gorgeous I want to gasp here in the serene cool waters. Instead, I manage a snorkel smile, flashing it at my hunky tour guide, but I don't linger on him for long, because a school of butterfly fish zips past us at Mach Speed.

A few feet away, a quartet of bright yellow tangs swims in and out of the rocks.

It's official. I'm converted. Sebastian the crab was right—it's better under the sea.

Serene and beautiful, and so out of my comfort zone, but Caleb sticks near me the whole time, and that's all I need to feel safe.

We surface with a splash. I want to crow with excitement, but I still have the snorkel in my mouth. I might cry with relief too—not so much that I survived but that I *loved* it. I feel bigger somehow with this new experience.

I remove the mouthpiece and slick my hair back from my face as I grin at Caleb bobbing beside me. "That was *incredible.*"

His smile is dazzling, even after the spectacle of the reef. "Amazing, right? Easily a few thousand white-spotted damsels."

"That's what they're called?" I ask. It's charming. "That's a great name for a fish."

"And we just swam right through them."

"It was just like you said—beautiful and somehow both peaceful and exciting at the same time."

He beams like I've made his day. Maybe his week. "I'm glad you liked it. I'm glad you tried it."

"You know what?" I confess. "I am too."

"So . . ." He tilts his head, exaggerating the delay. "That's score one for the snorkel lover?"

"I thought it was just"—I wiggle my eyebrows—"the lover?"

I mean for it to be teasing, and it is.

But it's flirty too.

He meets my gaze, still grinning, all confidence, all in with the flirt. "That works too."

* * *

I pile into the tour's shuttle bus with the rest of the group and flop onto a seat near the front. We are a tired, happy gang. People compare notes on the fish they spotted, chattering until Caleb picks up the microphone.

His grin is contagious as he meets the eye of each guest. "Hope you all enjoyed the snorkeling. I know it was new to some of you, so thank you for being . . . *ocean-minded.*"

Lots of groans at that, as there should be. Then a man from the back pipes up, "Well, they do say happiness comes in . . . waves."

More groans, and then I top it off with "All you need is vitamin . . . sea."

I get boos and hisses too, so I count that as a win. Especially when Caleb looks at me and smiles warmly before he gazes out at the group again. "And that concludes our afternoon trio of ocean-centric puns. Thank you very much. We'll be here all week."

We will. And as Caleb shoots me one last smile before he turns his focus to the road, I couldn't be happier about that.

6

CALEB

I park in front of the Marriott, the first drop-off, hopping out to stand at the bottom of the steps as most of the guests shuffle off. "See you all tomorrow. I'm expecting you all to be prepared for zip-lining."

A man on his way out says, "I've done a lot of zip-lining, but I've never had to prepare for it. How should we do that? Practice hanging in trees on the beach?"

"Absolutely," I tell him. "That's one of my top three tips for zip-lining."

The man laughs and says, "See you tomorrow."

I jump back on, close the door and slide behind the wheel. There's still one guest left— Skyler's hotel is the farthest out, so she's the last stop.

She moves up to the first seat as I put the

bus in gear, and we drive in comfortable silence as if we're both enjoying the quiet after all the excitement of the day. After a few minutes, she says, "Seems like everyone had a good time."

I glance at her from the corner of my eye. "And did you have a good time?"

"Absolutely," she says, heartfelt. "Except that now I want to know—what *are* your top three tips for zip-lining, Mr. Tour Guide?"

"Easy." I count them off by lifting my fingers from the wheel. "Know how to use the brake, don't put anything in your pockets you wouldn't want to lose, and ask yourself if you truly want to livestream your ride . . . or if you'd rather, I dunno, enjoy it in real time."

"So much to contemplate on the ride to my hotel."

"Don't get too deep. I'll have you back in ten minutes."

"Super." There's a private-joke spark in her mood. "If I return before six, I can order the DoorDash special."

"Oh no. Let me guess—you met the cabbie who moonlights as a delivery driver?" I ask, cringing.

"Yes. How did you know?"

"He's infamous around here. He's pretty harmless, but he does like to put himself out there." I shake my head. "What'd he offer you?

The island special? An eggplant with a serving of sausage?"

Her laugh lights me up. "He apparently can get me the most amazing fish and"—she lowers her voice, all faux sexy—"a little something on the side."

This time, I laugh. "I am not allowing you to risk a rendezvous with the infamous DoorDash cabbie. We're taking the scenic route." I pretend to slow for a turn. "Ah, look at the side road. Time for a detour up the hill. The views are great."

Skyler laughs. "Stay on course, Mr. Tour Guide. You don't have to worry about that. I'm actually on a man-batical."

This woman just keeps getting more intriguing. "I presume a man-batical is exactly what it sounds like?"

"You got it. It's like fasting, but with dates."

That sounds terrible, but then I remember Mia. "Huh. That doesn't sound like a bad idea, actually."

"Oh? You could benefit from getting off the wagon, romantically-speaking?"

"I think I defaulted into a dating detox."

"How come?" she asks, and it's all too easy to answer her—all too easy to tell her things about myself.

"My last girlfriend wanted too much, too soon. See, I have this theory that a relationship should follow a certain pattern. You should date. You should take your time. You should see how things develop." I catch Skyler smirking at me like I've said something funny. "What?"

"You're a rules guy," she says, definitely amused.

"What? Me?" *It's only been one day. How does she know this?*

She sits back, folding her arms, all smug and adorable. "I'm calling it. You're totally a rules guy. Reading people is part of my job."

"And what job is that?" I ask, curious. "Are you a matchmaker? A librarian?"

"No, although I do like the idea of combining the two and setting people up on blind book dates," she says. "I'm a personal stylist. I read people, size them up, and figure out what'll look good on them."

"Intriguing. What'll look good on me?"

She studies me, tapping her chin, then says, "Ask me after a drink and I'll have a better answer."

"I'll hold you to that," I reply, but I'm not interested in clothes. I *am* interested in that drink, however. "By the way, I'm not really a rules guy. I just like strategy and preparation."

"Exactly. And you have rules you go by for those things, right?" she teases.

"I'd call them more like *procedures* . . ."

She laughs.

"*Protocols,* maybe?" I ask, trying it on for size.

"Okay, Mr. Thesaurus," she says.

"Fine. If I am a *rules guy*—is that a bad thing?"

She shrugs. "No, but I think you like to do things by the book. I bet you always follow a recipe. And there's nothing wrong with that."

"Well, obviously. Because that's what a recipe is for—steps to make the food turn out and the cake rise." I glance her way. "You don't follow recipes?"

"I do not."

"How do you cook?"

"I don't."

I wrap my head around that, then point out, "Then, you're not *not* following a recipe."

"Oooooh," she says, like I did something naughty. "You just broke the double negative grammar rule. Maybe you're not such a rules guy after all."

We've reached her hotel. The drive went by too fast.

I stop the shuttle to drop her off, set the brake, and turn in my seat to face the intriguing former snorkel hater. "On that note, I will see you at eight a.m. sharp."

She does another of those sassy salutes. "Aye, aye, skipper. O-eight-hundred hours. On the dot."

But she doesn't move.

Neither do I.

I want to linger in this moment where it's just her and me and all this potential stretching out between us.

"Well, thanks for the ride," she says at last. "I mean, I know you had to give me a ride. It's sort of part of the package. But thank you. I appreciate it."

"It *is* part of the package, but you're welcome. I also enjoyed it." I'm damn glad she isn't staying at the same hotel as the others. "It's fun talking to you, even if you like to give me a hard time."

"But you can take it."

"I can indeed." Another pause, and then I make myself say, "Good night."

"Good night, Caleb." She slips out of the bus, and I watch until she's through the doors into the hotel.

Then I drop my forehead to the steering wheel with a *thunk*.

Why? Why, oh why, does she have to be pretty, witty, and totally endearing?

I thunk my head again, hoping to knock some sense into myself.

I know better than to enjoy her company this much—in this way.

It's one simple rule, man. Just follow it.

7

SKYLER

Thanks, universe.

For testing me like this.

For dropping a hottie tour guide IN MY PATH.

I flop down on my bed, groaning in . . . frustration.

But is it true annoyance? It's more like frustration meets lust. What's that called?

I grab my phone, click on my texts with Katie, tap out a note.

Skyler: Is frust a thing? Lustation?

Katie: Ah, so you are hot for the tour guide and it's driving you crazy!

Skyler: It's like you speak my language.

Katie: Yes, language of the weird and wonderful. Also, since you're texting me, you've clearly
not been eaten by sharks or fish. Yay!

Skyler: It's a vacation miracle.

Katie: And how did it go? You're not dead, but
were you hooking up with your movie star tour
guide? If so, I expect a FULL report.

Skyler: I won't be hooking up with anything
but a zip line. But I had so much fun today.
Everything was amazing. The snorkeling, the
reef, the fish . . .

Katie: And the sexy skipper? Sidenote: Skipper
sounds silly.

I laugh, then read her question again. Yes,
Caleb is easy on the eyes, but he's also easy to
talk to. And that counts for something.

Skyler: Yes, it does. Actually, I really enjoyed
his company. Maybe my vow of singlebacy
takes the pressure off so I can just enjoy talking
to him. He's interesting and fun.

Katie: Or, crazy idea, maybe you like the guy.

She's not wrong. I kinda do . . .

Skyler: There's a lot to like. But I'm also exhausted, and Caleb is picking me up at eight sharp. Tomorrow is zip-line day. I'm excited and terrified.

Katie: You're going to have fun. And I'm really proud of you for doing something that scares you, sweetie.

Skyler: Thank you. I'm proud of me too.

Katie: And have fun when Caleb picks you up

Skyler: The SHUTTLE BUS is picking me up.

Katie: Whatever you say, sweetie.

Skyler: I say GOOD NIGHT, Katie.

* * *

I wait for the shuttle bus under the portico in front of the Hilton. The butterflies in my stomach are for the zip line, not Caleb. I am not dating, this is *not* a date, and so these can't be date butterflies.

So why am I disappointed that the guests from the other hotel are already aboard the bus when it pulls up?

Caleb, however, doesn't disappoint when he

opens the door and stands at the bus steps as I trot over to join him. I'm not sure I've ever seen anyone make a Hawaiian shirt look as good as he does with those shoulders. The print could be inspired either by the sea and sand, or by his blue eyes and his golden tan and blond hair. It's a toss-up.

"Morning," he says, then glances at the bus as if checking on the passengers. When he looks back at me, he hands over the travel mug he'd been holding at his side. "Here you go."

"Oh!" I take it gratefully. "I didn't expect the tour to provide coffee."

His eyes crinkle at the corners as he grins. "We don't. But I thought you might like it." Then he leans over to whisper, "Shhh. Don't tell the others. I didn't bring enough for the whole class."

I whisper back, "Thank you. Secret coffee is the best. Just for me."

And I can't help but like that he's thought of this just for me.

* * *

The bus takes us up the mountain to the zip-line place, and then it's a trek up well-kept paths to the launch platform. The view of the ridges and lush tropical forest is breathtaking, and that's before I think about the trip down.

But there's one view I'm not nearly close enough to, so as the group climbs the trail, I fall back to walk beside Caleb, who is bringing up the rear.

"Thank you again for the coffee. It was fantastic," I say.

"You're welcome."

"I think coffee is proof we weren't meant to be morning people."

"I love mornings."

"You would."

He swivels his head to me, a look of mock horror twinkling in those ocean eyes. "What does that mean?"

I grin. "Mornings are for rules guys."

He comes to a full stop on the trail, and I do too. "And do you dislike rules guys?"

I make him wait a bit on my answer, delivering it with a tease of a smile. "I don't *dis*like rules guys who bring me coffee."

"Tsk. Tsk. *That* was a double negative."

"Which means it was a positive. Just like rules can be a positive too." I gesture from his sexy, broad shoulders down to his tanned, muscular legs—purely to demonstrate a point, of course. "Like, I bet you have a rule about daily exercise."

"As a matter of fact, I've already hit the ocean for my morning swim."

"See? Rules. You have rules."

"You call them rules, I call them strategies. Strategies to keep fit, strategies to keep guests safe and happy . . ." He glances at my hands as if I still held the travel mug I'd drained on the drive up here. "I bet *you* have a rule that you have to have coffee before the day can begin."

"I'd say that's more of a survival strategy. Still, a point to you." I lick my finger and draw a tally mark in the air.

Caleb chuckles. "Very sporty of you, for someone who doesn't like sports."

"You're making it easy for me to like things I didn't expect to," I say, soft, almost in a whisper. Goosebumps coast down my arms, and he opens his mouth as if to speak, but one of the other tour members falls back to ask him a question, effectively cutting the moment short.

Which is a good thing. I'm not here for moments. I'm here for discovery and adventure.

It's quite a hike up to this place, which makes me worry it will be quite a trip down. Still, I'm not nearly as nervous as when I boarded the tour boat yesterday, and the reason is walking beside me.

As the other tourists surge ahead once more, it's just Caleb and me at the back.

"Did you bring me coffee because I'm the only one who hasn't gone zip-lining before?" I ask him.

He looks at me in obvious surprise. "Um, no. I thought . . ." Running his fingers through his hair, he tries again. "I just wanted to, and I thought you would like it."

That little bit of nerves warms me as much as the gesture. "I do like it. Coffee is life."

"Same. Coffee is on my top five list."

"Top five . . .?" I prompt.

"Top five best things ever."

When he doesn't offer more, I say, affronted, "You can't just put that out there and then stop. What are the other four?"

Counting on his fingers, he says, "A good book, a beautiful wave, a burger and a beer, and yada yada yada."

Well, hello. "By yada yada yada, I assume you mean . . ."

"Laundry," he says, dead serious. "What else could I possibly mean?"

"Ah yes, of course. Laundry. How silly of me to think you meant something on the side."

"Maybe 'something on the side' is on a list all of its own."

"That's better than ranking it behind laundry."

"Depends a lot on your partner." He glances my way, and our eyes connect and hold. Heat rushes to my face, but he looks away first.

I clear my throat and redirect. "But let's

discuss this burger and a beer item. That's two things."

"They are a pair," he counters. *"Together* they're one of my best things ever."

"I dunno," I say. "That sounds like rationalizing. Two things can't be one thing. That should be against the rules."

"My list, my rules."

Caleb flashes me a grin that's almost as blinding as the sun on the water.

I will not be tempted . . .

Okay, I can't help that I am.

I will not give in to *temptation.*

"So, Mr. Rules Guy," I say, diverting the topic twice in as many minutes. "I took what you said yesterday to heart and decided to refrain from recording my zip-line experience."

"I approve. But that's my personal rule, not an official one."

I shake my head. "It's not about the rules. It's what you said about enjoying the experience in real time. And I intend to enjoy every second of it. I want to be totally in the moment."

"Then you'll love it," he says.

Caleb turns to me as we reach the starting point. The staff of the zip-line place are demonstrating harnesses and handing out waivers. I falter a little, because yeah, I'm going to voluntarily plummet off a mountain. That's a perfectly sane thing to do.

Caleb touches my arm as if to ground me in the moment, and tingles spiral through my body from the contact. "So, is there a particular reason you've never gone zip-lining before?" he asks, seeming oblivious to the effect he has on me. "Anything I should be aware of so I can make sure you have a good time?"

"Do you mean is there a snorkel story behind it?" I ask, trying to keep things light and decidedly *un*sexy.

"Exactly. Incidentally, your ex was a jerk. Just had to say it. When someone has never done something before, you don't just set them loose without giving them the basic guidelines. It's irresponsible at best."

"I appreciate that. And now I have a good experience to replace that disaster." *And with much better company.* "As for zip-lining . . ." I eye the cable that I'm about to trust with my life. "If we were meant to travel through the treetops, God would've given us wings."

He laughs. "You're a trip. So if we're not meant to fly over the jungle, why are you here?"

I glance from the launch pad to him and back again, then swallow hard. "That's a question to ask over a burger or beer, not before a girl is about to go down a zip line for the first time."

"My bad. Let's get you hooked in."

I eye the zip-line instructors up ahead. "Isn't that their job?"

Caleb shrugs, an impish smile lifting his lips. "It is, but for first-time zip liners, I like to guide them through the experience myself."

And when the guide is Caleb, I enjoy being guided far too much.

He helps me into an arrangement of webbing straps and buckles, tugging to test the fit. The double check seems meant to reassure me, which I appreciate. I *more* than appreciate it. The feeling is like the warm buzz of a secret cup of coffee, just for me.

When his hands run along the harness, a tingle slides down my chest. My gaze strays to those strong hands. Bet they'd feel good on me without this overcomplicated seat belt in the way.

Oh yes, they would.

I picture hands skimming along my arms, down my sides, over my belly, and my breath hitches.

"It's going to be great," Caleb says. "All you have to do is enjoy the ride."

I wet my dry lips. "I . . . uh, what?"

He nods to the edge of the platform. "The ride down the mountain. What did you think I meant?" he asks. His smirk says *caught ya*, but the heat in his eyes says either he read my mind or his is on the same track.

Maybe this is a top six item—enjoying lusty thoughts about my adventure tour guide.

The zip-line guy motions that it's my turn. Before I know it, I'm at the edge, with nothing stopping me from jumping but . . .

Me.

I can do this, I can do this, I whisper to myself, my eyes closed, my heart pounding against my ribs.

"You can do this, Skyler." Caleb's voice is close to my ear. "All you have to do is jump."

And so I do.

8

CALEB

It's been a long time since something made me happier than this—Skyler's gleeful scream as the zip-line whisks her away from the platform and over the valley. Even after countless times, the feeling doesn't get old—the swoop in the stomach, the zing of the cable, the rush of wind in your face. Plus, the magnificent view.

There's a pretty magnificent one in front of me now too. Skyler sits across the table from me at one of the reliable restaurants near—but not too near—the island's hotels. After we dropped the other guests back in town, we made it here for that burger and beer—to prove a point. Simply to show her why this is one of the top items on my list.

We give our order—burgers and beers—and Skyler gushes about today's adventure until the latter arrives, and she stops to take an appreciative sip and then sighs.

"Thumbs-up on one of your items," she says.

"Half of an item," I amend, and we both settle in a bit with our drinks.

"All right," I say. "Beer is here, burger is on the way. Now . . . what's the story with this trip?"

"First, I want to know where your love of . . . *strategy* comes from."

I shake my head and sigh. "I'm not going to convince you I'm not a rules guy, am I?"

"Let me think," she says. "No."

"Fine. I'm not conceding that I am, but here you go. I loved sports as a kid, and all kinds of games. Board games, like Monopoly, and sports like soccer, and absolutely anything I could do in the water. I competed in swimming, water polo . . ."

"I can see why you think in terms of strategy then."

I shrug. "So, I approach life the same way, I suppose. If you want to play the game, you need to follow the rules."

She nods. "That makes sense. I get that. I feel like I get you now, Caleb." She pauses, tilts her head to the side. "Does that seem strange?"

"Not at all," I reply, because funny thing—I think she does. "Now it's your turn. Tell me about the trip."

"I was originally going to take a trip to do spa-type things. It's my single-versary."

"Ah. Single for a year?"

Holding up a finger, she clarifies, "Voluntarily single."

"Of course. Hence the celebration trip."

"Thank you! Finally, someone gets it." She leans her elbows on the table, beer glass between her hands. "I needed a break. I was in a relationship a year ago that became a little too all-consuming, and I kind of lost sight of myself. So, I've been working really hard not to do that again."

I nod, because I do get it. "Hence the man-batical. But that's great that you recognized what you needed and did that for yourself."

"Exactly." She takes another sip of beer then places it down on the table. "Your turn. What's your dating story?"

"It's sort of the opposite of yours. As I said, my ex wanted too much too soon. And honestly . . ." I grimace. "She got a little clingy."

Skyler tilts her head, curious but not judging. "What happened?"

"Like early on, bringing sweet rolls from a local bakery to my home office one morning was a surprise treat, you know? But then it was lunch several times a week, then it was *homemade* lunch . . ."

"Hmm," she says. "That sends a very domestic message."

I nod. "That and the constant hints for an invitation to everything I did or anywhere I went—I hardly knew *her* and she wanted to be an *us*."

"That's it!" Skyler sits up straighter. "I am trying to know *me* before I'm part of a *we!*"

I grin. "That's brilliant."

And I can't help but think how lucky someone will be to pair up with someone so confident in herself. That's the kind of woman I want.

One day.

"Enough about exes," I say, before I get myself in even deeper. "Thing is, I really shouldn't even be having a drink with you."

"Ooh." She leans her chin on her fist, sexy and adorable at the same time. "Are there rules against hanging out with a customer?"

"If 'hanging out' is code for *hanging out*, then yes. We should definitely not be . . ." Her gorgeous pouting mouth is enough to make me forget what I'm saying. "Hanging out."

She's leaning closer over the table, or maybe I am. "No . . . *something on the side?*"

"Definitely, absolutely no *something on the side*. No side, no starter, and especially no dessert."

"Here are your burgers." The waiter's interruption is the best and worst thing to happen. Skyler and I both sit straighter as he sets our plates in front of us.

"Thanks, man," I say.

"Let me know if you need anything else."

He vanishes as Skyler and I trade glances. She presses her lips together as if trying not to smile. I'm not a mind reader, but a good tour guide learns to anticipate a guest's needs, and I suspect hers would coincide with mine just now.

I nod to her plate. "Let me know if you think this is a top five."

She takes a bite and makes distracting, delicious noises. "Yeah, I can definitely see why this is on your top five list. But what about waves? You'll have to explain the appeal."

"You'll see when we go surfing tomorrow."

"Surfing? Tomorrow? In the ocean?"

"Surfing lessons. The ocean is kind of a requirement."

"Did I tell you that tomorrow I'm missing my alarm and sleeping in all day?"

I love her sense of humor. At least, I hope that's humor. "You did look at the schedule when you signed up, didn't you?"

"Of course. Things are just different in the . . . abstract. Thinking about a boat versus getting on one, for instance."

She's not wrong. Thinking about my rules when she's not around? It's a no brainer.

But with this gorgeous woman in front of me, tempting me, smiling at me, it's hard to stop my *hands off the client* rule from flying out the window.

I need to remind myself who she is—someone who could decimate our business with a terrible review.

Someone who's eventually going to leave.

"You remember when you first arrived, Ms. Professional Shopper, I asked what would look good on me, and you said you'd tell me after you'd had a beer?" I ask, successfully changing the subject from intimate to abstract.

She shakes her head, dabbing her mouth with a napkin as she finishes a bite. "Can't. It would be against the rules to tell you."

"Personal shopper rules?"

Another shake of her head, slower this time, her eyes holding mine. "Your rules. The no side, entrée, or dessert rule."

I swallow, unable to stop myself. "Go ahead and tell me." How bad could it be?

"Well . . ." Pink flares across her cheeks. "Nothing."

I frown. Her blush doesn't match the word.

"Nothing would look good on you."

Ohhh. Now I get it.

"As in . . . nothing at all?" I ask, just to be

sure.

"Yes. What's underneath all your clothes. *That* nothing." She smiles, a little devilish, a little naughty, and holy hell, that's my new favorite smile. "My professional opinion is that nothing would look good on you."

I should resist, and yet I've zip-lined past resistance. She's too fun, too flirty, too fascinating. Right now, she's turning me on *too much* for me to care about rules. "*Only* your professional opinion?"

She shrugs one shoulder. "Happens to be my personal opinion too." There's a hint of *come up and see me sometime* in her voice, and I like it.

"Well, Skyler," I say, quieter, more secretive. "I happen to think nothing would look good on you too."

She keeps her gaze locked on mine, and her eyes say she wants me to break the rules. Her words, too, when she says, "I told you that my answer would break the rules."

"But we're not breaking them . . . tonight."

The waiter appears using whatever stealth technology lets him sneak up on us like that. "So . . . dessert, anyone?"

Skyler and I lock eyes again. *Dessert.*

She breaks first.

While the woman dissolves into laughter, I tell the confused waiter, "No, thanks. We really can't."

9

SKYLER

As the stars flicker in the Hawaiian sky, I stand on my balcony, staring at the water, Face-Timing Katie.

Full reports are required.

"I had a burger and beer with Mr. Hot Tour Guide, and it was one of the top five evenings I've ever had. We talked about everything, and then we flirted, and then I may have told him he would look good in . . . nothing."

Her eyes twinkle with dirty thoughts, that turn to dirty words. "On a scale of one to movie star, how *is* his birthday suit?"

"Oh hush. I can't give that a rating, because I haven't seen it. And I'm not going to see it, because it's against the rules. And he's a rules guy. Plus, that's not the reason I'm here."

"Blah, blah, blah. I feel like I should be supportive and say something affirmational about your willpower, like, 'Yes, stay true to your man-batical.' But I can't." She brings her face closer to the screen, and stage whispers. "Because I've seen the tour company's Instagram feed."

"You stalked their Instagram?"

She nods as she stretches on her couch. "One, it's not stalking, it's appreciating their social media marketing. Two, it's in the friend code. Rule three, section five, provision ten: thou shall check out all potential suitors and render a Verdict of Suitability. Assuming he's the one with the dark-blond hair, perfect cheekbones, and those eyes . . ."

I sigh happily. "As blue as the ocean."

"Then my verdict is—break the rules."

I shake my head. "Nope."

"Okay, then. Bend them. Because provision eleven dictates: thou shall report back to said good friend on all rule-breaking activity while on a tropical island. It's the Tropical Tryst Addendum," she says, with a wink.

As an island breeze gently blows my sundress, I say, "First, the Tropical Tryst Addendum would have to state that one's friends *should* engage in tropical trysts."

"Exactly. It's an addendum. Follow it!"

"You are such an enabler," I tease, moving from the balcony to the lounge chair, as the waves lap against the shore in a gentle night-time whoosh.

"That's also in the friend code. Especially for friends who might not enable themselves and might need a push."

"I guess I'm a rule breaker then. Because I'm going to break that rule and not have a tropical tryst."

She sighs, dejected. Then takes a deep breath, gives me a more intense stare. "But seriously, just tell me why this is a bad idea. You like him. You can have a conversation with him. You flirted with him all through dinner."

Her questions are good and valid, and yet, a fling would be risky. "Because flings are the type of thing that I started the single-versary fund to avoid. Because he has a clingy ex. Because he lives in Hawaii and I'm all the way over in San Francisco."

"Look, all of that is true, but you're stronger than you think. You started the fund and fulfilled the fund. That was the hard work. Now you can enjoy yourself. It's not falling back into old habits. It's having fun. And you deserve fun."

Maybe she's right. Maybe it's not as risky as I think. But there's another issue. The *how*. There are other people around us pretty much all of the time.

"I'll think about it," I say.

"Good. Because I think you deserve a fling. That's not the enabler in me. That's the true friend."

I smile, glad that she is precisely that.

* * *

No one mills around on the beach near my hotel this morning.

Well, plenty of people lounge and splash, but none of our tour group. And I didn't see anyone as I walked over.

Just the guide, leaning against a fence and looking good enough to eat, or at least lick all over.

Metaphorically.

Caleb straightens as I reach him.

"Hi. Um. Did I sleep through a zombie uprising last night that took out the rest of the tour?"

He grimaces, which doesn't bode well. "You could say there was an uprising, yeah." At my confusion, he explains, "It was the halibut."

"Zombie halibut?" I look toward the waves in horror. "And you think I'm going to go in the water for this surfing lesson?"

Caleb laughs. "I didn't think it was possible for you to want to do this *less*."

I glare at him. Not really, but kind of.

"Undead fish, Caleb. Going in the water with live ones is difficult enough."

"No zombies were involved at all. It was the halibut the rest of the group had at their hotel. The 'something on the side' was a case of food poisoning."

I cover my gasp of sympathy. "Oh no! How awful for them."

"How lucky that we had burgers," he says.

"*Those* burgers might be on *my* best things list now."

"Agreed. Anyway, it's just you and me today."

"Oh. It is?" My voice climbed an octave. "Okay . . ."

"Are you sure?"

"Of course!" I say, too brightly. I'm bordering on chipper, actually. "Of course it's okay."

He eyes me suspiciously. "Yeah?"

Yeah, except for the temptation-athon that is unfolding before me. It's going to take all my willpower not to invoke the Tropical Tryst Addendum.

"Sure," I say in a more normal voice. "It means we can skip the surfing lesson and go shopping. I saw some super-cute boutiques in the downtown area."

I start to turn, but Caleb catches my arm,

which is the opposite of helpful in the temptation department. "Not so fast."

"Yes, this fast. That sounds like a perfect day."

"Let's make a deal. I give you a surfing lesson and then you can give me a shopping lesson. But I'm not going to wear . . . nothing." His mouth curves in a rule-breaking smile. "Unless you're super convincing."

I suck in a breath at the idea of what I could do to convince him. "You are evil. And fine, I promise not to tempt you with birthday suits."

"Well, you don't have to *promise* . . ."

"Yes, I do. I'll never keep to the rules. So, focus on something else. Anything. Even . . ." I pretend to gag. "Surfing."

We go over to where he has two surfboards stuck in the sand.

Like really tall tombstones.

"Let's start with the basics of surfing etiquette."

"Like what side of the board the fork goes on?" I quip, and Caleb laughs.

"More like share the water. Don't cut in. Don't hog the waves. Observe the right of way . . ."

"This sounds a bit like driving lessons. Nobody likes Driver's Ed, Caleb. But people really like shopping."

He shakes his head. "Is there anything you won't do to try to get out of this?"

"Of course there is. Everyone has their limits."

"Well, aren't you here on your single-versary to push yours?"

Suddenly the beach is a lot hotter.

"I promise this is easy," Caleb reassures me. "Grab your board and let's go."

I don't carry my board so much as drag it toward the surf, following Caleb into the shallows. He stops when the water is waist-deep and turns to me. "We're going to start by just lying on the board. That's how you're going to get a feel for it."

Following his example, I pull myself onto the board lengthwise on my belly. "I think this might give me a feel for napping in the sun. I'm down with that."

A chilling spray hits my back. Caleb splashed me! I shriek and roll off the board. I pop up again, wiping water from my face. "Hey!"

"Still feel like napping?" he asks with a smirk.

"Not so much." I shake my head, flicking him with water. "Might as well surf."

His mouth widens into a grin. "That is music to my ears."

* * *

For the millionth time, I fall off the board—gravity and the waves are conspiring against me. And for the million-and-first time, I haul myself back up onto it and lie on my belly.

I can just do this for a while. I'm good at this part. Or I can paddle to shore. I got the hang of paddling pretty quickly. Caleb says I'm A-plus at paddling. I tell him he's an A-plus teacher.

And he is.

"Just keep doing it," he says after five hundred wipeouts. And when I get myself back on the board: "That's it. Just keep getting right back up. Eventually you'll get the hang of it."

"This is my final attempt," I tell him, calling over the waves. "After this one, I'm going ashore."

"You keep saying that," he calls back. "But you keep getting back up. You're doing great."

The swell of a wave looms closer. I get ready, boosting myself to my feet, into position.

"That's it," Caleb says. "You're doing it! You're riding the wave!"

I am! I am totally upright and moving forward. I'm showing the ocean who's boss!

Look who's out of her comfort zone now.

* * *

I barely have the strength to drag my surfboard out of the water. As soon as I do, I fall to my knees in the soft sand and flop onto my back. A minute later, Caleb stands beside my prone body.

"I did it," I pant. "I actually surfed for a full two seconds."

"You did!"

"I told you that was my final attempt."

"Technically, it was your first success."

I shade my eyes so I can see his smile—no, his damn proud grin. "What did the trick for you?"

"Thinking that we would go shopping next if I got that one right."

He laughs and shakes his head. "A deal is a deal."

"I know where my talents lie."

He holds out a hand to help me up. "So, come on. Impress me."

* * *

We take Caleb's Jeep downtown, where I get my second wind as soon as I'm in sight of the shops.

"Now," I say, rubbing my hands together, "it's my turn. Your lesson in shopping." Caleb walks along the sidewalk beside me, a good sport but unenthusiastic. "What do you hate most about clothes?"

"Shopping for them." His gaze turns heated as he looks at me. "Sometimes wearing them."

"Hmm . . . I can see you'll be a hard one."

"Hard indeed."

I bump him with my shoulder to get him to behave, but it brings home—again—how muscular he is, and it makes me imagine—again—what those arms would feel like around me.

This attraction has gone from temptation to nemesis.

Focus on something else, Skyler.

"Right. Well, to help ease you into the experience, you can watch me shop like a professional first."

10

CALEB

The only thing I enjoy about shopping is Skyler's gorgeous new sundress.

No. Her new sundress with a spectacular Skyler in it.

The rest is a haze of boutiques and dressing room doors that might as well revolve, she comes out and goes back in so many times. Everything looks nice on her, and then—whammo—she walks out in this sunshine-yellow dress that shows off her tanned shoulders and hints at her breasts and reveals those strong legs, and I can't breathe.

Nor do I need to again, I'm convinced.

I can subsist off the view of this woman.

I've thought she was gorgeous from the moment I saw her on the dock, but getting to know her, watching her get up on the surfboard again and again? She's breathtaking.

We grab dinner, and as we come out of Sunset Bob's, Skyler says, "Thanks for dinner. Shopping makes me hungry."

"Are you sure it wasn't the surfing that made you hungry?" I ask.

"It was definitely the shopping."

I chuckle, even though I knew she'd say that. "Have I mentioned you look spectacular in that sundress?"

"A few times." She smiles. "But it's nice to hear." We start toward the Jeep, neither of us seeming in a hurry. "You know what's spectacular?" she asks, tucking a strand of hair behind her ear and gesturing to the orange and pink sky flaming up above us. "That sunset."

"Yeah. It never really gets old. Funny how it happens every day, and every day you can't look away from it."

"Do you want to go down to the beach and watch the sunset?" she asks, her voice soft. "Or is that against the rules?"

I scoff. "Watching the sunset is never against the rules. And in the Hawaii rule book, it's a requirement."

Her eyes twinkle up at me. "Then we'd better do it. Or else."

"Just a couple of rule-abiding citizens."

On the beach, we don't hurry, and we don't talk much either. The shush of the waves is a gentle soundtrack.

Skyler sighs, sounding wistful. "This is magical."

"It is," I agree, in the same I'd-like-to-stop-time way. "Some mornings I wake up early and go outside and watch the sunrise. And it never fails to reset me."

"Right? Like, it reminds you everything will be okay."

"Exactly. The sun rises, the sun sets, and it's gorgeous every time. Because every time it brings new possibilities."

"New things you can learn," Skyler says.

Neither of us is looking at the sunset. Instead, I'm looking at the beautiful woman across from me, the sunset setting her auburn hair on fire, the gentle breeze sending waves of goosebumps over her skin.

"New people you can meet," I say.

"New experiences with new people."

"First kisses," I say. I catch myself and clear my throat, and, well, I have no strategy for this. "I know this is against the rules, but you look really beautiful against the sunset. And it's not just because of the dress, or because of the sunset. It's because you're you. I really like talking to you."

"I like talking to you too," she says. She wets her bottom lip. "But I'd also like . . ."

I step closer, curling a hand around her hip. "First kisses that are also sunset kisses?"

Her breath hitches. "I wonder where that would be on the list of best things."

Another inch—I'm officially in the kissing zone now, and there's no place else I'd rather be. Especially when she lifts her chin and parts her lips.

"I suspect it would be off the charts," I reply, but I more than suspect. I know it.

Her eyes twinkle like she knows the same thing. Her arms wind around my neck, and yeah, we fit just right. "Let's find out," she says, so damn seductively that I'm done for.

Rules? What rules?

Closing my eyes, I dip my head to capture her mouth in a kiss. Her soft, lush lips brush against mine, her island scent swirling around us as we explore each other. Tongues skate, hands skim, soft sighs mingle.

She tugs me closer, and I comply, hauling her against me, ramping up the kiss, deepening it, savoring her.

Her murmurs tell me to keep going, and who am I to deny either one of us *this*—a sunset kiss.

Yes, kisses are just better at sunset, with the ocean lapping the shore, the breeze caressing our skin, and the island setting the mood.

That mood is—don't stop.

So we don't.

We kiss and then kiss some more, and soon, she's not only gone to my head, she's filled my mind. She's my only, all-consuming thought.

And I want to kiss her everywhere.

But first, I need to pause for breath, if only to refuel with oxygen.

Skyler's eyes are closed, her expression blissful. When her lashes flutter open, she lets out a dazed, "Whoa."

"'Whoa' is right."

She blinks at me then the sky. "What time is it? Is that the moon?"

I glance up as if to check. "I do believe it is. Which means we've been kissing for, I dunno, an hour, give or take."

Our arms are still looped around one another, and her fingers play with the ends of my hair. "So, I have a thought."

"I'm having several." I tug her more firmly against me. "We should see if they match up."

Now her fingers thread through my hair. "I'm thinking of invoking the Tropical Tryst Addendum."

"Tell me more. Because this sounds like a rule I'm into already."

"It's an exclusion in the Dating Hiatus Decree. See, since I'm leaving in a few days, and since you live here, and I live—"

I don't need to hear any more. "I don't live

here, but that's beside the point. If you're suggesting we break the rules for one night, my answer is yes. An infinity of yeses. Screw the rules."

"Then let's get out of the comfort zone."

11
———

SKYLER

We don't even bother with the bed.

The second the door of my hotel room snicks shut, Caleb crowds me against the wall, and yes, I like alpha Caleb very much.

I like when he grabs my wrists, pins my arms over my head, and slams his mouth down on mine.

My head is a static haze of want.

My body aches.

My pulse throbs in my chest and in my throat and between my legs.

Touch me now, take me now.

I want to scream those words, but he's devouring my lips, consuming my mouth, and it's all so mind-bendingly good.

So worth breaking the rules for.

As he fucks my mouth with his tongue,

Caleb lets go of my wrists and snakes his hand up my skirt, right where I want him.

His fingers glide over the wet cotton panel of my panties. A groan rumbles from his chest as he breaks the kiss. "Oh yeah, you definitely need me to break the rules."

"I do," I say breathlessly. Desperately.

He grabs his wallet from his shorts pocket, produces a condom, then hands it to me.

My brow knits. "Um . . ."

Then I shift to an "Oh" as Caleb strips in seconds flat.

And hello.

He's even hotter naked.

Like, tropical-island-dream hot.

Like so damn sexy I want to watch him walk out of the ocean, all ripped muscles and wet hair and thick cock.

"Happy vacation to me," I say, wrapping an eager hand around his length.

He shudders, groaning as I stroke him, then he slides his hand inside my panties again, stroking my clit. I shudder, pleasure already rolling through me, as if the time we've spent over these last few days—talking, teasing, trying new things—has been all the foreplay I could ever possibly want.

As tension coils inside me and I grow close, closer still, he pushes my hand away. "Need to get inside you, Skyler. Now," he commands, and same. Same here, Caleb. Let's go.

I give him the condom, hurriedly stripping out of my dress and panties as he covers himself. As soon as he does, he grabs my thigh, wraps my leg around his hip, and rubs against my wet center.

"So good," I gasp.

"So fucking good," he answers, then he sinks inside me in one delicious thrust.

My world spins off its axis.

This is too intense. Too yummy. Too fantastic.

It's out of my comfort zone but totally in my *yes, more, give me more* zone.

Caleb drives into me, clasping my leg tight around him, filling me then pulling out to fill me again. With each thrust, waves of pleasure crash over me until I'm panting and moaning.

With my arms roped around his neck, I drag him as close as he can get as he fucks me against the wall.

"Harder," I beg.

And this man with the body carved by the outdoors gives me everything I want—a good, hard tropical tryst in my hotel room, ignoring every rule.

Exquisite bliss is just out of reach. It's almost here. And I want it, and like he senses what I need, he drops a hand between my legs, stroking me as he drives into me just so.

Just right.

It's so damn good that I break apart in ecstasy, the night, the trip, and the no-man-plans fading away.

"Coming," I cry out, and he growls in my ear, groaning through his own release before he stills, shudders, then sighs.

Sighs as deeply and happily as I do.

12

SKYLER

Light filters through the hotel window, but I float in a luxurious fog between "Hey, it's morning" and "I'm on vacation." The bed shifts with a rustle of sheets, and I remember every detail of why this morning feels so decadent— he's stretched out beside me, propped on one elbow.

"Hey, sleepyhead," Caleb says, all rumbly voiced and sexy.

I smile lazily. "Hey, yourself." Then I notice he's dressed, and I switch to a pout. "You're going?"

"I need to get out of here to get ready for Hanging with Sea Turtles. I'll see you in a couple hours, and let's pretend I didn't fall asleep in a customer's hotel room."

"News flash . . ." I stretch my arms over my

head with a satisfied purr. "You did more than fall asleep."

"Mmm . . ." He leans over for a kiss. "Keep making that sound and I'll be late."

I reach up to curl my fingers in his hair. "Turtles are slow. You can catch up."

Even his chuckle makes my toes curl. "Not really the point, but still a good one."

"I won't tell your boss you're moonlighting as a deliveryman for multiple Os. Thanks for making mine a double, by the way, with one on the side."

"The pleasure was all—well, equally—mine." With one last, quick kiss, he rolls out of bed in one move, like it's that or not leave at all. I wouldn't mind, but can see why that would be a problem.

"Don't worry about telling the boss," Caleb says, making sure he has his phone and wallet. "He already knows, since the boss is me."

"You are?" I sit, tugging the sheet up with me.

"Yes. I own the company." He glances at me, curiosity in his expression. "Does that bother you?"

"Um, no. Just surprised." I don't know why that didn't occur to me. His experience shows, and I definitely saw his bossy side last night. "How long have you been in business?"

"I started the company about seven years

ago, but I've been leading tours since I was twenty-three. I was on the swim team in high school and college, but competitive swimming wasn't a career path."

"Seems you found another path into the water though."

"I can't seem to resist the sea. Or the pool. Pretty fond of showers too." His eyes roam downward as if he's imagining the things we could get up to under the spray. Then he drags himself back to the topic. "But anyway, yes. I studied business so I could actually do something with my aquatic skill set."

"So, not only are you sexy and funny, you're also smart *and* strategic." I study him, my head tilted to match the new angle I'm seeing him at. "Explains why you have all these rules."

He shrugs. "It's good business practice."

"And you need to set the tone."

"Yeah." After a thoughtful pause, he sits on the side of the bed. "But you know how you wanted to get out of your comfort zone?"

"Which I did—with your help."

"Well, with you, I want to break the rules. So how would you feel about breaking them again tonight?"

"Invoke the Tropical Tryst Addendum once more?" I grin. The answer is easy. "I'd say yes times infinity."

* * *

Time for a full report.

Once he's gone, I grab my phone and tap out a text. I tell Katie he's a spectacular kisser, that the sex was wall-banging, toe-curling, sheet-grabbing bliss, and that he's the owner of the company.

And thinking about him, makes my fingers fly over the keys.

Skyler: In some ways, he doesn't seem the boss type. He's all Hawaiian shirts and board shorts. He's ripped from doing stuff he loves to do, and he has this understated confidence that in the bedroom is just *whoa*. You know?

Katie: Uh, I'd like to.

Skyler: It was the kind of night and the kind of sex that makes you want to move to a tropical island and fall in love, forget you even have a job. And . . .

Katie: And what? I'm staring at three dots and dying here, Sky.

Skyler: Oh, shit. I can't. I can't go there.

I sit up straight, heart pounding in worry as I re-read my texts. I sound hung up. I sound lost in a man.

And that's everything I want to avoid.

13

CALEB

I saunter into the office, fresh from the shower, fresh cup of coffee in hand, fresh day of island life to enjoy. A peppy song playing during the drive from Skyler's hotel bops through my head until Brady suddenly spins in his desk chair to stare at me.

"What?" I ask, running a hand over my hair and clothes to check for stowaway lizards or insects. It's Hawaii. Aloha.

"You're whistling."

"Really?" I didn't realize that. "Sorry. Earworm."

He shakes his head, studying me with narrowed eyes. "That's not an earworm whistle. That's an extremely-satisfied-with-my-life-right-now whistle."

That's both accurate and insightful. I'm not

a grumpy guy, but my mood is *unusually* content.

Brady leans back in his chair, steepling his fingers like an obnoxious know-it-all. "Well? Did you win the lottery, or did you get lucky the other way?"

I exaggerate a prim look of disapproval. "A gentleman does not kiss and tell."

"That's a yes, obviously." He drops his pose, seeming just the normal amount of curious. "Is this a one-time thing or a many-time thing?"

"I really like this woman. She's kind of awesome, and I'm seeing her again tonight."

My friend breaks into a delighted smile. "Good luck to you, then. Where'd you meet her? Tinder, Match, Bumble . . .?"

"Uh. Well . . . ahem . . ." I open my laptop, suddenly fascinated by my email as I mumble, "None of the above."

"No, dude!" He throws back his head and rubs his hands over his face. "Just no. You did not."

I try to feel bad about it, but I can't. "Yes. Yes, I did. Sorry, not sorry."

He laughs incredulously. "Don't apologize to me. It's your company and your rules. I'm just shocked because you're usually so adamant about them. You seriously slept with a client?"

"Yup." I consider the last few days with

Skyler. "And, in retrospect, maybe went on a couple of dates."

"How do you date in retrospect?"

I shrug. "It seemed like just enjoying her company. Appreciating getting to know her better."

"That's exactly what dating is."

I shoot him a doubtful stare. "I don't know about you, but for me, not every enjoyable conversation ends up in bed."

Brady tips his head as if to acknowledge my point, then taps his pen on the desk in an anxious staccato. "Look, I'm not one to butt in—"

When I'm finished laughing, he continues. "But you're my friend, so I have to ask—didn't you end up dating Mia without knowing it?"

A prickle of unease starts up my neck. "Only from her point of view. I knew where I stood."

"Fair enough." More pen tapping. "And you're technically my boss, so I'm just going to *mention* the Travelocity-slash-Expedition-Tours fiasco."

The prickle becomes more of an icy tingle even as I protest. "This isn't the same thing at all. Skyler has no expectations, and she's not vindictive."

"Cool, cool. As long as you've considered the ways these things can go sideways. It's what you'd tell the guides, so now I'm telling you."

My buoyant mood sinks like a punctured pool float. "I do say that." I have these rules for good reasons, which are all rushing back to me now.

Brady leans forward in his chair, elbows on his knees, his expression earnest. "Look, you may decide this woman is worth the risk. Just think it through. It's not like you to be cavalier about this stuff. You've always put the business first."

"You're right." I run my hand down my face. "This is my business. Everyone who works here is counting on me."

It was one thing to throw out the rule book while caught up in sunset kisses. But in the light of day? That's not strategic. That's not me.

"I'll cancel tonight," I say. "Better to quit and hit the reset button than drag things out. Skyler will understand."

"Just tell her something came up with work and you have to bow out."

I like Skyler too much to lie to her. But it's not entirely untrue. Something did come up with work—all the reasons why I have these rules and why I should never break them.

* * *

That's a lot to set aside while I do my job today. Especially since my job includes the distraction of Skyler in the flesh—flesh I'm well acquainted with after last night. Add in worry about hurting her feelings and whether I should think anything about the text I received just before I left the office . . .

Skyler: Hi. I decided to take the hotel van to the Marriott so you only have to make one pick-up this morning. Makes it easier for everyone.

I am ninety percent sure she did it because everyone is still feeling queasy after the fish apocalypse. The other ten percent gnaws at me as I welcome the tour guests onto the shuttle.

"How are you holding up, Mrs. Smith? Glad to see you on your feet, Mr. Cooper. Looking fantastic this morning, Mrs. Wainwright . . ."

I turn from giving the older woman a hand up the steps, and there is Skyler, waiting to board.

"Oh, hey there. You look fantastic too."

"Thanks. I appreciate that."

I frown at something in her tone. "Is everything okay? You seem . . ."

Tired?

Distant?

"I'm great." She sounds cheery, but a little like she's reading from a script.

"So, about tonight . . ."

Yep. I'm about to make things worse.

"Tonight?" she echoes.

"I have to cancel. There's a meeting—something's come up at work."

"Work has a way of doing that. Don't worry about it."

There's still something off about her tone, but I let it go as she climbs onto the bus. We have a schedule, and I have a guilty conscience, so possibly I'm projecting.

Standing at the front of the aisle, I grab the mic, smiling a welcome at all the guests. "Good morning. I'm relieved to see you all pulled through. Count yourselves as true adventurers, having faced adversity and survived to tell the tale."

"Trust me, this is a fish tale you don't want to hear," groans Mr. Cooper. The heckling is weaker today, but still a good sign that he's on the mend.

"You are absolutely right about that," I say. "I thought we'd keep it low-key today, so we'll postpone the sea turtles and visit a couple of waterfalls this morning."

At their murmurs of approval, I slide into the driver's seat and put the bus in gear, adjusting the mic so I can finish my spiel. "Some of the falls on the island are breathtaking, and this is one of my favorite sites. You don't see waterfalls like this where I'm from in

California. I hope you'll feel as wonderstruck as I am every time I visit. For now, just sit back and enjoy the scenery."

But even though I love Hawaii, even though island life is what I live and breathe for, something about the scenery seems lacking as we hurtle toward the final few stops on the tour.

14

SKYLER

California?

That's what he said. *Where I'm from in California.*

Why am I reeling from this? Everyone is from somewhere.

But it was like I only had to follow one hallway, then someone threw open an unexpected door that led to more doors and now I have all these chances to choose the wrong one.

When the bus stops and the passengers exit and disperse through the park, I hang back while Caleb directs the guests toward the trailheads and lookout points. As soon he returns to the shuttle, I pounce.

"You're from California?" I ask.

He blinks, startled, and yeah, I meant to ease into that a little. But now that I've jumped, I have to follow the zip-line down. "Like, you were raised there and moved here?"

"No, I live there," he says. "My friend Brady handles most of the operations on the island, and I focus on California. We have a lot of adventure tours there too. I was going to mention it last night, but I got . . . *distracted*."

My skin heats in a blush that spreads up my neck and across my chest, and memories have stolen my breath. "Same here. I think I was distracted too."

He ducks his head a little closer and says softly, "I think you still are."

I *am* distracted, it's true—flustered by his smell and his warmth and the golden-sand color of his hair and the surf-blue of his eyes. "I'm fine. Totally fine."

Tilting his head, he studies me as if I'm a puzzle. "Is that a problem, me being in California?"

"*I* live in California," I blurt. "San Francisco. I mean, it's not like you live in San Francisco. Right?" Why can't I stop talking? "It's not as if we both happen to live in the same place. What would be the odds of meeting somebody on an island and it turns out that they're practically neighbors by California standards?"

I try to laugh at the whims of fate, but it comes out slightly maniacal. Desperately, I wrap up with "So, you must be from someplace else?"

Caleb's expression has gone from surprise to bemusement to neutral . . . ish. "Yeah. I'm in San Diego. So, not someplace we're going to keep running into each other."

"No, of course not. I mean, we're totally not going to keep seeing each other. That would be silly."

There's a beat where we're both surprised I said that, then Caleb recovers with a forced-sounding laugh. "Yeah, that would be ridiculous. That's not what we talked about."

"Not even remotely. None of this"—I gesture from him to me—"is about anything but here and now. I didn't even know you were from California. It's not like I met you and thought, 'Oh my God, I'm going to meet somebody, and we'll date when we go back to California, and everything's going to be fabulous.'"

"Of course not. You wouldn't be thinking that, because you're on a man-batical. And *I* wouldn't be thinking that, because of my ex and work and all sorts of things."

"Exactly. And I'm not going to go all *stage five clinger* on you. I'm totally not like that."

"So, California is irrelevant. You might as well be from a foreign country," he says, nodding as if to convince me, or maybe even himself.

"Right, totally. Absolutely. California is huge. We couldn't be farther apart."

Then, there's silence. I'd expect to be relieved, but, unbelievably, the heavy quiet between us is even more awkward than the talking.

Caleb breaks it first. "Except . . . there *are* flights."

My breath catches at the possibilities. "True. Pretty frequent ones, really. It's not hard to go between cities."

"A little bit of an effort, but not impossible."

"A little bit of planning *if* . . ."

But I'm not brave enough to say it.

"Yeah, *if* . . ." He swallows hard. "The big if."

Another silence, full of another kind of tension. "Except," I say tentatively, softly, "this was just a one-night thing on an island. Right?"

He holds my gaze and doesn't let go. "Well, two nights. It was going to be two nights."

I frown. "But you just canceled. Your work meeting."

He shakes himself as if coming out of a trance. "Right, yeah. The work meeting. Super important."

Try *super* unconvincing.

He lied to me—cancelled our plans because he didn't want to see me again.

A shock of emotion hits and leaves me with

two options: cry in front of him or get the hell out.

I paste on a bright smile. "On that note, I'm going to go check out some waterfalls."

Get the hell out it is.

CALEB

Alone in the shuttle, I groan and scrub my hands through my hair. "Caleb, you idiot. *Work meeting?* What was I thinking?"

I catch the sound of a footstep and snap my head toward the rear of the bus. Mrs. Wainwright stands in the aisle, one hand on the back of a seat for balance. Her hair is mussed, but her eyes are bright.

"Mrs. Wainwright?" I choke on surprise and chagrin. "Where did you come from?"

"Right here." She waves to the seat beside her. "Buses always put me to sleep. And then your conversation was so cute, I thought, who's going to notice an old lady napping?"

"Okaaaay." Where to even start to . . . explain? Apologize?

She takes the decision away from me. "It's obvious you two have it bad, but you don't know how to let the other know, so you're acting all weird. You should tell her you want to see her in California."

"But I don't," I insist.

She tuts, and I feel five years old. "You won't help matters by lying to me or to yourself. You just need to sort things out in your relationship."

"Mrs. Wainwright, I'm afraid you have the wrong impression. We're not in a relationship. We're just having a . . ."

Her penciled eyebrows arch. "A vacation fling?"

I wince at how that sounds, especially from someone who looks like my grade-school librarian. "It's a tropical tryst between two adults without expectations. And it ended. Amicably."

She gives me a long, pitying *you poor, deluded man* kind of look.

"I wouldn't count on any of that. That woman is your girlfriend-to-be." She leans in and whispers conspiratorially, "Just a heads-up, dear. I'm pretty sure she knows the 'work meeting' is a load of horse apples."

Then she pats my hand and goes off to view the waterfall.

16

SKYLER

"Welcome to the Coconut Café." The hostess smiles at me from near the restaurant door. "How many in your party?"

After a year, you'd think I'd be used to this, but it stings a little more today than it should. "This is my party. Party of one. Happy to dine alone."

The young woman's smile widens just a tad. "Wonderful. Would you like a table outside? There's a fantastic view of the water."

"Sounds perfect."

One last night to enjoy the ocean vista.

The hostess leads me to a table on the patio, offering me the menu. "A server will be by shortly. Enjoy!"

What's not to enjoy? There's a breeze and a view and tropical scents in the air.

The server appears beside the table. "Hey

there. Can I get you anything while you wait for your—"

"My phone," I say, cutting him off with a smile. "I'm having dinner with my phone."

"Oh. I'm so sorry. My apologies."

I wave them away. "It's fine. Truly." I came here on a single-versary. One last night having dinner for one is more than fine—it's good.

Yup. I am all good.

"Would you like a Coconut Mai Tai? It's quite excellent with the edamame appetizer."

"Why not?" I'm just living on the edge tonight. "When in Rome, as they say."

He thanks me for my order and leaves, and I take out my phone and open a text.

Skyler: Hey. Want to have appetizers with me?

Katie: How sweet of you to ask. How were the sea turtles?

Skyler: We saw waterfalls instead. Look.

I share the pictures I took this morning, which she exclaims over in unironic emojis. As my drink and appetizer arrive, I snap a selfie holding the mai tai. A year ago, I would have thought that was sad or brave, but now, holding up my phone while I toast myself amid the tables full of couples and friends, I feel good. This is me.

Katie: Beautiful. *chef's kiss*

Skyler: Thanks. I've really enjoyed my adventure. Even the surfing. Shhh, don't tell anyone, but I might try it again.

Katie: Aha! I knew it. So, was it the bikini? Was it magic?

Skyler: I think I was just ready for a change.

Katie: I'm not surprised. Do you feel any different?

Skyler: I do. I never would have tried some of these things before. I wouldn't want to LIVE on an island. But I'm glad I came here . . . even if the tropical tryst didn't last. It lasted exactly long enough.

Katie: Seems to me like you've been getting out of your comfort zone for a whole year. You focused on you. You poured your energy into your business and your friendships and health. This trip wasn't to prove anything, but to celebrate all that.

Skyler: You know, I think you're right. And when I see Caleb tomorrow, I'm going to say thanks and move on.

The waiter approaches me and my electronic date deferentially and asks, "Was everything to your liking?"

I nod, thinking beyond the meal to what's ahead. "Thanks. Everything was exactly what I wanted. And what I needed."

17

CALEB

"Whoa. You look like hell," Brady comments from the doorway as I slump in my chair.

"Thanks," I grumble. "I didn't sleep much."

"No shit." He approaches with exaggerated caution and puts a cup of coffee in front of me. "What's on your mind?"

"I fucked up everything yesterday." At his panicked look, I clarify, "With Skyler."

"Awkward."

"No shit," I echo.

"Listen, mixing work with pleasure is never easy. Let me cover for you. Get some rest. Go sleep in a hammock or read a book on the porch."

It's tempting. I don't want to avoid Skyler. I want to avoid seeing her hide her hurt with distance.

"I should do the final day."

"Nope. Overruled." He grabs his tablet and checks the tour's details, then pauses to look at me full-on. "And listen. Maybe have a longer think about this woman and your rules. Maybe she is worth breaking them for."

I stare at him agape. "You're a sleep-deprivation illusion, aren't you? Where is yesterday's Brady?"

"Right here." He fusses with the screen some more. "I still think mixing business with pleasure is a bad idea. But I'm not you. And you want to know the best thing about owning your own business?"

"Surf breaks at noon?" I ask, but my voice doesn't hold its usual enthusiasm.

"No," Brady replies. "It's that you get to make the rules, and you get to change them if they no longer suit."

Change the rules?

Change them so dating a customer . . . might indeed work?

"Now, this pathetic moody funk of yours will infect the passengers, and that's bad business too. So, I'm kicking you out of here for the day. Goodbye. Shoo. Farewell. Aloha."

He's dead right—kicking me out is a very good idea.

18

SKYLER

Caleb isn't here, and I don't know how I feel about that.

Rather, I do.

Disappointed. Confused.

But I'm not sure what that means in relation to my resolve from last night.

Mrs. Wainwright and I cross the beach—this one rockier than the ones marked for swimming. "Look!" she says, and we stop. "There's one sunbathing on a rock."

I smile at the sight of the turtle. "It's funny because you don't think a turtle sunbathing is something you ever want to see in your life, then you see it, and all you can think is 'How did I ever live without seeing a turtle sunbathing?'"

The older woman absolutely beams at me. "Yes! That's exactly what I was thinking."

"That turtle is actually known as Don Juan," says Brady, Caleb's sub. He introduced himself to us all on the bus.

I look from the turtle to the guide, skeptical. "Don Juan. Is that so?"

"I call BS," adds Mrs. Wainwright.

Brady raises his left hand, the right one over his heart. "Swear. He's fathered, I kid you not, one hundred baby turtles."

My eyebrows shoot up. "Huh. Single-handedly doing his part to un-endanger the species."

"It's a tough job, but someone has to do it," Brady says.

We watch a while longer, looking to spot another.

"Oh!" I gasp, and point at the waves. "Look! A baby turtle swimming!"

We watch it as long as we can and all sigh happily. "I officially declare turtles the coolest ever."

Mrs. Wainwright says, "I second it."

"Third it," adds Brady.

I glance at my companions and then back out to the water. "Also, at the risk of being cheesy and TMI with strangers, this is exactly what I needed to be doing today. Does that make sense?"

"It's not TMI," Mrs. Wainwright decrees. "It makes perfect sense, and it's just as I expected."

"What?" I glance at her in confusion. "What do you mean?"

Brady interrupts, clearing his throat. "If you ladies will excuse me for a second . . ."

Then, Brady walks away.

19

CALEB

I don't lounge in a hammock.

Or chill out as I watch the waves.

Instead, I swim. And as I push through the ocean, I think.

About the last few days.

About the past.

About rules.

I think about all the walls I've erected. The boundaries I've set in place to protect my business.

But really, to protect me.

To protect my heart.

Trouble is, they didn't truly work. My heart's already in this. Crazy thought, but so it goes. A few days with Skyler and I already know—I want more days with her.

I want flights, I want planning, I want the big if.

I want to know if she thinks we can be more than a fling, since I'm pretty sure we can be a whole lot more.

When I get out of the ocean, I dry off, and head for my Jeep, driving toward another swath of beach. After I cut the engine, I make my way quickly along the sand, as my phone flashes with Brady's name. I answer right away, but before I can get out a *hi*, he says, "Dude. You're a dumbass if you let this woman leave. End of argument."

That's quite an about face. "Who is this? What are you doing with Brady's phone?"

"Don't listen to the stuff I said before. She's cool. She loves turtles, and she's chatting with this other woman, and she gets along with everyone, and . . . *she loves turtles*," he says, sounding enchanted for me.

I feel enchanted too. With Skyler.

"Told you she was great. I spent the morning going for a swim in the ocean, and all I could think was how foolish it would be to let her get on that plane without telling her something I just realized," I say, sparks of excitement whipping through me as I picture Skyler, as I imagine reconnecting with her.

Telling her what's on my heart and mind.

"You better get here soon, since we're almost done."

I grin as I walk past rock and sand, around a curve on the beach. "Good thing I'm walking toward her now."

Actually, it feels like a great thing.

20

SKYLER

I look for Brady, but he's gone. When did he leave? I didn't notice him take off.

But I can't miss the man walking toward me across the sand.

Caleb.

"Hey," he says when he reaches me. "Can we talk for a moment?" He glances at Mrs. Wainwright, then back at me, gesturing over to a rocky outcropping. "Maybe over there where it's a little more private?"

I think the older woman snorts, but I'm too curious about what Caleb has to say to do anything but agree to his suggestion.

We stroll away from the others without talking—not until he stops to face me.

"Skyler," he says seriously. "I have a confession. I didn't have a meeting last night."

I laugh in surprise. "I figured that out."

His rueful expression is endearing on his handsome face. "I was a little freaked out by how much I wanted to see you again," he admits. "And then I had a realization while I was in the ocean earlier."

"I hear time in the ocean can be as useful as time with a life coach."

The corner of his mouth lifts. "This was definitely a life-coachy moment. And here it is—sunset kisses are one of the best things, but *only if* they lead to more than a tropical tryst."

I am . . . cautiously intrigued. "Is that so? What sort of *more* did you have in mind?"

"The sort of *more* that says it might be a challenge to date someone in San Francisco when you live in San Diego. It'll definitely take effort, and meticulous scheduling. It requires planning, and planes. But . . ."

He doesn't finish, and I don't know how he'll complete the sentence, only how I want him to. "But what, Caleb? Is this another *if?*"

"*No.*" He's confident. Certain. "There are no ifs. No ifs at all.

No ifs at all." He slides his arms around my waist. "If you think about it, all that planning will be a lot like snorkeling."

I arch a questioning brow. "Dating me is like snorkeling?"

"Yes, as in, worth it." His hands curl around

the small of my back, tugging me closer. "Was snorkeling worth it?"

"Snorkeling was the perfect way to spend a day. Sort of like watching sunbathing turtles."

"Ah, so you're saying dating *me* is sort of like spying a sunbathing turtle."

I smile, a little teasing, a little inviting. "I can't think of a higher compliment."

"In that case, Skyler, would you like to continue this tropical tryst? Maybe turn it into something more? Because I really hope you'll break your man-batical for me."

I shake my head. "I would, Caleb, but I can't. I'm not on a man-batical anymore. I broke it with you, and I'm one hundred percent fine with that. I want to see where this takes us."

"Let's see if it takes us into a stateside steady zone."

And steady zones need kissing. So I lift my face to his and plant a kiss on those yummy lips. A warm Hawaii kiss that makes my toes curl and my chest flip. He moans softly as I slide against him. Smiling, I tug him a little closer, savoring his reaction and getting a little more lost in his kiss.

A familiar voice interrupts from a few yards down the beach. We break apart.

"Oh, how romantic!" cries Mrs. Wainwright, clasping her hands in front of her. "I know you're busy—sorry, not sorry—but I just have to say something to Caleb."

"What's that, Mrs. Wainwright?" he asks politely.

She thrusts her arms in the air, dancing a victory jig. "Called it! I told you she was your girlfriend-to-be."

"Actually," he says, still with his arms around me, "I'm hoping she wants to be my girlfriend *right now.*"

And I do, so I say, "Unless Don Juan makes a better offer, I'm game."

EPILOGUE

Skyler

Months Later

Katie kicks me out of her town car at the San Francisco airport.

Well, lovingly kicks me out.

"Go, go, go," she urges. "I've got a yoga class, and you've got your man to see."

I slide out of the back seat. "Thanks for the lift."

"What are friends for?" I throw my arms around her in a quick hug, then I stare at her engagement ring when I let go. "And we're dress shopping soon."

She beams. "I can't wait. I'm over the moon

to marry him," she says of the guy she met a few months ago. One whirlwind engagement later, and here she is—almost hitched.

"And I can't wait to be your bridesmaid," I say.

"Go have a fabulous weekend," she says.

I take off, knowing I will, grateful, too, for all her support and friendship.

Glad I can give the same back to her.

* * *

I could make my way to the San Diego airport's pickup zone with my eyes closed. I wheel my suitcase behind me just as a car pulls over to the curb. The door opens, and the ruggedly handsome driver gets out.

"Need a lift?" Caleb asks with a grin.

"Sure. Can you take me to this guy's house? I have a tryst with him in, oh, about twenty minutes."

"I bet I can get you to his house in fifteen," he says, taking my bag and adding with a cheeky grin, "I'm highly motivated."

This I could do on autopilot too—getting in the car, clicking my seat belt. But I wouldn't want to miss what comes next.

Caleb reaches over the console and cups my cheek, his eyes loving, his voice gentle. "Hi. Missed you."

"Missed you too," I say softly, leaning into his touch. "So much."

"Good to see you. For the—what is it now? The twentieth time in six months?"

"Yes, but who's counting?"

He runs his fingers through my hair. "Evidently, me."

The car behind us honks impatiently.

"All right," Caleb grouses at the other driver. "Keep your shirt on." I giggle, and we exchange smiles. "That's my cue to get you home."

He puts his hands on the wheel, but before he puts the car in gear, he pauses. "You know, if this were your home too, I wouldn't have to keep counting your visits."

I gasp, scandalized. "Why, Caleb, are you asking me to have another tryst?"

"Let's see. We've had the tropical tryst and the city tryst." He slides a glance my way. "What if we had a live-in-the-same-home tryst?"

I'm delighted but not surprised. This is Caleb. Things happen with him with perfect timing—not too early and not too late. It's one of the things I've grown to love about his *strategic* way of doing things.

"Hmm," I purr, sliding my hand up and down his thigh as he drives. "As long as it comes with the 'something on the side' special."

He catches my hand and kisses it. "Always, Skyler. You always get the Double O special."

"Then I say infinitely yes."

THE END

Eager for Katie's story? It comes next in **A Wild Card Kiss** when the jilted bride meets a sexy single dad sports star on what was supposed to be her wedding day!

Order now and read on for a preview!

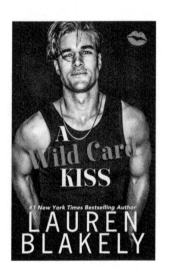

Harlan...

"Elvis Presley is in the house!" I shout as I crank up the volume to "Hound Dog," and Abby lifts her chin to howl at the moon.

I clap, keeping rhythm as my six-year-old uses a wooden spoon as a microphone, crooning along with Elvis's tune.

She breaks off to grab a rubber spatula from the flour-and cherry-covered kitchen counter. "You need a mic too, Daddy," she says, thrusting it at me.

I take the instrument and we slide into our best imitation of The King as we wait for the pie to bake.

We finish our daddy-daughter duet as the timer bleats, and Abby points wildly to the oven. "It's ready! We can eat it now."

I laugh, shaking my head. "You know the drill. You've only made, what, ten million pies with me? We have to let it cool."

"Ten million and fifty!" She bats her lashes. "But I was just hoping maybe this time."

I ruffle her curly brown hair, chuckling at her attempt to make me bend. "Hope is a good thing, little bear," I tell her as I turn off the timer. "But pies don't cool with hope. They cool with time. Also, you know this pie isn't for us." I grab a Rudolph the Red-Nosed Reindeer potholder, open the oven door, and slide out the cherry pie. I set it on a rack on the counter, then use my hands to direct the scent of sweet and tart fresh fruit and crumbly crust our way.

"It smells so good," Abby says, bouncing on her toes as she inhales.

"Course it does. We made it. We rock. And your mom is going to love it."

Abby arches a mischievous brow. "What if I eat it all first?"

I bend to drop a kiss onto her nose. "Then you're going to have the biggest bellyache in all of San Francisco," I tell her, then rub her tummy.

"Fine. I'll wait. But I hope she lets me have some tonight," she says with a touch of worry. "I really, really hope so."

Ah, the dilemmas of youth.

I worry whether this city's NFL team will offer me a contract next season and if I'll even want it, whether my kid is making friends at school, and whether she'll want to find a new gymnastics class, since she decided to quit the one she was taking.

She worries about pie.

It's a fair tradeoff.

An hour later, we're ready to go. I grab a pie box from the stash I keep, pop in the tasty treat, and tell Abby to find her overnight bag.

It's bowling night with the guys, so I'm dropping Abby at her mom's house. I don't always bring pies, but Danielle and her hubs dig them, so I try to do so as often as I can. Also, it does *not* suck making pies with my little girl. Win-win.

Abby snags her panda backpack from the

hallway and slings it onto both shoulders. "And now I am officially ready."

I swing open the door. "Panda is on the back so it's go time."

On the sidewalk, Abby reaches for my hand. I take her little one in mine and we head toward California Street.

She looks up at me, concern in her hazel eyes. "Are you sure you have to go to training camp next week?"

Okay, not all her worries are of the sugar variety. This kid misses me when I'm out of town, and I sure as hell miss her.

I throw her a them's-the-breaks smile. "I do. The Renegades won't let me play if I don't show up. But I'll talk to you every day."

"I know. I just miss you when you're gone," she says, matter-of-factly as we near the corner.

"I miss you too, little bear. Every day. And that's why I always call you from training camp, and away games, and every night when I'm on the road," I say.

She sighs, a little forlorn. "And I *always* can't wait for your calls."

Time to cheer her up. Remind her that we have a regular routine. That I'm around a helluva lot. Half and half—that's how the time split works with her mom. "Did you know I've been calling you from every single training camp since you were born? Even when you were *only* eight months old?"

Her expression turns intensely serious. "I remember that."

I bark out a laugh as we turn the corner. "You do *not* remember that. No one remembers stuff from when they were one. Or two, or three, or four, or five, for that matter."

"Well, I'm six," she says, like I don't know her age. Like I need the reminder of how seismically my life changed that November day more than six years ago. When she was born, this little bundle of joy and chatter and brightness upended my days and nights, and I learned in an instant what it means to love someone so much it hurts. It hurts so good to love like this.

"I am well aware that you're six and sassy. But still, you don't remember me FaceTiming you from the Paleolithic era."

She crinkles her nose. "What's pale licks?"

"A long time ago. When dinosaurs roamed Earth."

"Daddy!" she shouts in a fit of laughter. "I'm not that old and you're not either."

"Oh, I'm pretty old. In football years, I'm definitely a dinosaur. But not a T-rex, because they can't do anything with their teeny arms," I say, flapping my left arm like it's as useful as a big dino's, while holding the pie high in my right hand like it's a football.

Abby's eyes widen to pizza size. "Be careful!"

I thrust the box even farther away with my outstretched arm. "Did you or did you not see my one-handed, game-winning catch in the Super Bowl this year? My second Super Bowl win, Miss I Remember Everything."

But she's lasered in on the pie, and only the pie. Back to sugar worry. "I just *really* don't want you to drop the pie."

"And I *really* didn't want to drop Armstrong's thirty-three-yard pass," I say, taking her back to that beautiful day in February. "So I didn't." I put her out of her misery, hauling the pie box back to my chest. "Better?"

A long sigh of relief is her answer. "I've been waiting all day for that cherry pie. But it feels like I've been waiting a year."

"I know what you mean, but it'll be okay. Promise," I say. Because kid time is eternity.

We weave past a goateed guy pushing a sleeping toddler in a jogging stroller.

The guy stops. "Taylor? Harlan Taylor?"

"That's me," I say, hoping he's a fan, not a hater. We have our share of both in this city. Any team does, and you never know who you're going to run into.

But the dad breaks into a wide grin, pressing his hands together in a prayer. "Thank you for that catch. But please re-sign this year. If we lose you to another team, I will die."

He's exaggerating, of course. But he sure does sound like he'd be devastated if I went elsewhere in free agency. But it's not up to me. I have no idea if the Renegades will re-up with an ex-running-back-turned-receiver who's nearing the end of his playing days. I'm thirty-six, already on the long end of a long career.

"I'll do my best to make sure you live," I tell the fan as I offer my free palm to high-five. He smacks back, then continues on his way.

Abby and I do the same.

"It's weird that you're famous," she says, reaching for my hand and swinging ours together again.

I scoff. "I'm not famous."

"Please, Daddy. Don't be silly. You're sooooo famous. All the kids at school say so."

"I'm only *kind* of famous. And only locally. And only with sports fans."

"That's still famous, then," she insists, and I can tell I won't win this battle with her, so I relent.

"Fine. You win."

"But you don't seem famous when we're at home," Abby points out.

"Good. That's how it should be."

Soon, we turn onto Danielle's block and head up the front steps to her Victorian home.

Abby pushes the doorbell, but Danielle's already swinging open the red door, letting her in.

"Hey, cutie-pie," she says, scooping up our daughter and peppering her cheek with kisses. Then to me, she says, "Hey, you."

"Hi, Danielle. I brought you your favorite pie."

"Cherry!" She makes grabby hands. "You're a godsend. Jamie and I have friends coming over tonight, and I was going to rush out to the bakery and grab a cake."

"There is never a need for cake when you have me around," I say, then make my way into her home.

Her husband looks up from the dining table where he's drawing a pig, or maybe a duck, or possibly a cat, with their two-year-old.

"Hi, Harlan!" the little kid shouts.

Jamie lifts a hand. "How's it going? You ready for your last season?"

My mind snags on the word *last.* Is he trying to trick me into confirming the rumors?

Love the dude, but I swear he's got a bet with his buds he'll be the first to reveal what I do at the end of the season.

Hell, I'd like someone to reveal it to me.

Danielle comes to the rescue, setting a hand on her husband's shoulder. "Honey, you're a broken record. Maybe find a new topic."

Jamie shoots her a confused look, his gray eyes narrowing. "Like what, sweetheart? The new surgical technique for reattaching a retina? And football is starting soon. Football *is* the topic."

Danielle tosses her hands in the air. "How about the latest restaurants in Hayes Valley? Or maybe interesting tech news? Perhaps baseball?"

"Hmm, the new Thai place or whether the city's star receiver is going to stay or go . . . What's more interesting?"

Danielle shrugs helplessly. "Football fans. What can you do?"

Jamie smiles and stands, gesturing to the kitchen and the deck beyond. "You want a beverage, Harlan? Soda? Bubbly water? Beer? We're grilling later if you want to join us." He lowers his voice to a stage whisper. "We can talk about baseball. How about those Dragons?"

"They look good this season. Maybe they'll finally win a World Series," I say, happy to shift to another sport.

"Home run!" the two-year-old shouts.

"And a bubbly water would be great," I add.

"I'll grab it," Abby calls as she sweeps into the dining room, clutching an early reader book from among the many lying around. "And I like football better, Daddy."

As the girl joins her mother in the kitchen, Danielle pats Abby's head. "I wonder why."

After Abby returns with a raspberry LaCroix, I catch up with Jamie, chatting about the Dragons chances of making it to the Fall Classic. When we've shot the breeze for thirty minutes, I stretch my arms and tell them I need to take off.

Danielle walks me to the door, motioning for Abby to stay behind.

"Thanks again for the pie, and for the school check," she says softly.

"Of course," I say, but I kind of can't believe she's thanking me for paying for Abby's school. What else would I do?

"I appreciate it," she adds.

"Danielle. C'mon. It's a given," I say.

Her expression softens. "I don't take it for granted."

"You never have, and I never thought you would," I say, since friendly is how we do things.

I met Danielle at the University of Washington. We dated our freshman year of college, but then she transferred to a school with a better pre-med program. I ran into her again the night I won my first Super Bowl. She was at a post-game party, and we hit it off again. I gave her a hard time about her preferring the San Francisco Hawks over the San Francisco Renegades. Then I gave her a hard time between the sheets, and we said our goodbyes in the morning. A few weeks later, she learned she was pregnant.

A Super Bowl baby.

The Southern gentleman in me reared his head and asked Danielle if she wanted me to marry her.

I'd never heard a woman laugh so hard in my life.

"We're not in love. That was a one-night stand. No, sweetie. I just want to know if you're interested in helping raise this baby. It's hard being a doctor and a mom."

Was I interested?

Absolutely.

I wasn't going to be a deadbeat dad.

"Of course I am," I said.

"Are you sure? A lot of athletes aren't."

"I'm not a lot of athletes." Sure, I'd been the good time guy. I was still a helluva ladies' man back then.

But I also damn well knew what family was, thanks to my mom and the way she looked after all of us after my dad walked out.

I was not going to do that.

So, we agreed to raise Abby together as friends, as co-parents, and as equals.

A few years later, she met Jamie, a fellow

surgeon, and married him. Abby and I went to their wedding together.

Now, in the doorway, I give Danielle a serious look. "It's not only my job to take care of her. It's my pleasure," I tell her. "And you, if you need it."

Danielle lets out a sigh of relief. "I never want to assume."

"You're a sweetheart, even if you prefer the Hawks. Glad you're her mom," I say, then I cup my hand over my mouth and call to Abby that I'm leaving.

She runs over and leaps into my arms, clutching me like a koala. "Bye, Daddy."

"I'll miss you, little bear. But I'll call you tomorrow night."

"Just like you did when I was one." Abby stares up at me, her hazel eyes big and serious. "And I remember you sang Dolly Parton to me as a lullaby."

Holy shit.

Does my kid have a weird-ass memory from being an infant? How is that possible?

I narrow my eyes in suspicion. "Wait . . ."

Abby cracks up, swatting my shoulder. "Got you! Mommy told me you did that."

"Dolly's the best," Danielle adds.

"That she is," I agree, and then I tap Abby's nose. "Let me know if you want to do gymnastics somewhere else in the fall."

"I'm still thinking about it."

"Take your time," I say gently. But I know how much she loved it, so I hope she'll want to go again.

She looks away briefly, then nods, resolute. "I will. And I'll let you know. Promise."

"Love you, little bear."

"Love you too."

I say goodbye, humming "Nine to Five" as I make my way across the city to a bowling alley to meet my buds.

For the next few hours, I have a blast throwing strikes and gutter-balls alike with my friends until, one by one, they peel off. As the clock ticks closer to ten, it's just Cooper—my quarterback—and me, and we chat as we make our way out, passing the bar inside the bowling alley where my gaze catches on a woman in a formal white dress.

That's odd enough to rate a look, but something about her feels achingly familiar.

Possibilities nag at me all the way to the exit then won't let me leave.

At the door, I tell Cooper I'll see him at training camp. "I swore I saw someone who looked familiar. I'll catch you later. I need to go check on something."

He lifts his chin in a goodbye. "See you at camp."

I turn around, the blonde profile triggering a memory that tugs me back to the bar.

Could it be?

Is that . . . her?

A tingle of excitement coasts over my skin at the mere possibility.

When I reach the bar, I take a deep breath and look in, then I shake my head in amazement.

The woman in white is none other than someone who, seven years ago, I desperately wanted to see again.

And she's wearing a wedding dress as she orders another shot of tequila.

Grab **A Wild Card Kiss** now!

Be sure to sign up for my mailing list to be the first to know when swoony, sexy new romances are available or on sale!

ALSO BY LAUREN BLAKELY

FULL PACKAGE, the #1 New York Times
Bestselling romantic comedy!

BIG ROCK, the hit New York Times Bestselling
standalone romantic comedy!

THE SEXY ONE, a New York Times Bestselling
standalone romance!

THE KNOCKED UP PLAN, a multi-week USA
Today and Amazon Charts Bestselling standalone
romance!

MOST VALUABLE PLAYBOY, a sexy multi-week
USA Today Bestselling sports romance! And its
companion sports romance, MOST LIKELY TO
SCORE!

WANDERLUST, a USA Today Bestselling
contemporary romance!

COME AS YOU ARE, a Wall Street Journal and
multi-week USA Today Bestselling contemporary
romance!

PART-TIME LOVER, a multi-week USA Today
Bestselling contemporary romance!

UNBREAK MY HEART, an emotional second chance USA Today Bestselling contemporary romance!

BEST LAID PLANS, a sexy friends-to-lovers USA Today Bestselling romance!

The Heartbreakers! The USA Today and WSJ Bestselling rock star series of standalone!

P.S. IT'S ALWAYS BEEN YOU, a sweeping, second chance romance!

MY ONE WEEK HUSBAND, a sexy standalone romance!

CONTACT

You can find Lauren on Twitter at LaurenBlakely3, Instagram at LaurenBlakely-Books, Facebook at LaurenBlakelyBooks, or online at LaurenBlakely.com. You can also email her at laurenblakelybooks@gmail.com